ONE
Italian
SUMMER

ALSO BY KERIS STAINTON

Counting Stars
Spotlight on Sunny
Starring Kitty
Emma Hearts LA
Jessie Hearts NYC
Della Says: OMG!

For younger readers:
Lily and the Christmas Wish

ONE
Italian
SUMMER

KERIS STAINTON

HOT
KEY
BOOKS

First published in Great Britain in 2017 by
HOT KEY BOOKS
80–81 Wimpole St, London W1G 9RE
www.hotkeybooks.com

A CIP catalogue record for this book is available from the British Library.

ISBN: 9781471406386
also available as an ebook

1

This book is typeset using Atomik ePublisher
Printed and bound by Clays Ltd, St Ives Plc

Hot Key Books is an imprint of Bonnier Zaffre Ltd,
a Bonnier Publishing company
www.bonnierpublishing.com

To Alice, Hayley and Rachael. For always being there.
And to Stella, for literally being there (again).

1

'Do you want to dip your finger in Dad?' my older sister, Elyse, asks, holding out the small clay pot containing her share of our father's ashes.

'God, Elyse!' I shriek, jumping backwards.

'Elyse, no one wants to do that apart from you,' my younger sister, Leonie, says. She's got the same expression on her face as I imagine is on mine. 'It's sick and wrong,' she adds.

Elyse shrugs, screws the lid back on and puts the pot back on her bookshelf. 'I thought it might help.'

'Help how?' I ask.

'I don't know. It just makes me feel better and since you're all worked up about the flight . . .'

'I'm not "worked up" about it,' I say, as I look along Elyse's shelves for a book to take with me, but I can't see anything that's not about fashion or design. Partly for her degree – she's in her second year – but mostly because she's obsessed with it. 'I'm just not looking forward to it.'

'You didn't used to be bothered about flying,' Leonie says.

She's sitting on the floor next to Elyse's bed and painting her toenails black.

Now it's my turn to shrug. 'It's not the flying. It's everything. It's just . . . different this time.'

'First time without Dad,' Elyse says.

I nod. 'It's going to be weird.'

'We could take a photo of him and put it on the seat,' Leonie suggests.

'And that wouldn't be weird at all,' Elyse says.

'From the girl who sticks her finger in his ashes for luck?' I say. .

'Do you think I'll be able to draw on these with chalk?' Leonie asks, wiggling her toes in the air.

'Maybe,' Elyse says.

'But why would you want to?' I ask.

Leonie shrugs and then lies flat on the floor with her feet still up on Elyse's bed. 'I can't believe it's tomorrow. It's come round so fast.'

'I can't believe Robbie's not coming,' Elyse says, throwing herself back against her huge pile of pillows. She sleeps practically sitting up.

I stand with my back to the bookshelves, my hands behind my back with one hand holding onto one of the shelves. I look at my sisters: Elyse on the bed, Leonie on the floor, both of them staring up at the ceiling, which I know without looking features a constellation of glow-in-the-dark stars.

'I think it's better that Robbie's not coming,' I say, knowing full well Elyse will strenuously disagree. 'I think it's nice that it's just going to be family.'

Also Robbie gets on my nerves, but I know better than to say that to Elyse.

'And Luke,' Leonie says and tips her head right back so she's looking at me upside down. She waggles her eyebrows; it looks extremely weird. Luke. Our cousin Toby's best friend, who's out there working with Toby for the summer.

'Oh, yeah,' I say. As if I'd forgotten.

'As if you'd forgotten,' Elyse says and laughs. 'Fine for you if my boyfriend stays at home. Meanwhile you'll be all heart-eyes at Luke.'

I roll my (non-heart) eyes. 'Yeah, okay, I made a total arse of myself over Luke. Can we all get over it?'

'You didn't make a total arse of yourself,' Elyse says.

'Just a bit of an arse,' Leonie finishes, swinging her legs down and clambering up on the bed next to Elyse.

'Well, I won't be doing it again so we don't need to think about it any more,' I say.

And they don't know the half of it. I head for the door, but out of the corner of my eye I catch my sisters exchanging a glance.

'What?' I say, stopping with my hand on the door handle. 'Why are you looking like that?'

'We're just a bit worried . . .' Elyse starts. She stops and looks at Leonie.

'About Mum?' I ask, twisting the door handle in my hand.

'Well, yeah, obviously,' Elyse says.

'But about you too,' Leonie adds.

'Me? Why?'

'You're not yourself,' Leonie says. She's all tucked up with her chin on her knees and she looks closer to six than sixteen.

I sigh. 'I know. I know I've changed. But we've all changed. Since Dad . . .' I don't finish the sentence.

'We have,' Elyse says, nodding. 'Of course we have. It's just that you don't seem to be doing so well.'

'I'm fine,' I say.

They're both looking at me with the exact same expression of concern. They've each got the little line between their eyebrows just like Dad used to get. Most of the time they don't look that much alike – Elyse's face is round and her blonde hair is long and wavy, while Leonie's face is more angular and her dyed red hair is short and blunt – but they do when they frown.

'But you've stopped singing,' Leonie says.

I feel a clench in my belly. This again? 'I haven't stopped,' I say. 'I still sing. You've heard me sing.'

'Yes, but you quit the band and now apparently you're not going up to Liverpool . . .'

'I haven't decided that yet,' I say. 'Just because I haven't sent the acceptance back doesn't mean I'm not going.'

'Mum said you got a prospectus for UWL,' Leonie says.

'I did. But I haven't decided anything yet. I'm just being practical. Things are different now.'

'They don't have to be,' Elyse says. 'Not that different, anyway.'

'Do we have to talk about this now?' I say. 'It's my turn to make dinner.'

They look at each other again and then Elyse says, 'Fine. But we will talk about this again.' She takes her phone out and holds it right up to her face because she's not wearing her glasses.

4

'Are you setting a reminder?' I ask, appalled.

Elyse laughs. 'No, you stupid cow. I got a text from Robbie.'

'You're done then?' I ask. 'I can go and do dinner?'

'Yeah, go on,' Leonie says. 'I'm starved.'

'Good,' I say. 'And I am fine. Really.'

2

Mum's on lates this week at work – she's a doctor – and so we have a rota for making dinner: one night each for the three of us and then we can go out or get a takeaway. It works pretty well, even though we don't have that big a range. Elyse got a Jamie Oliver book out of the library so we can try to expand our repertoire a bit, but I'm sticking with turkey chilli for tonight. I can't face trying something new.

I've got the recipe stuck to the fridge with the letter magnets we've had for as long as I can remember. Dad used to leave messages for us with them. Sometimes just 'LOVE U', sometimes something daft that only we'd find funny. Mum doesn't do it. She occasionally leaves us notes on the fridge, but not with the magnets and not usually jokey. She's all practical these days.

I'm chopping onions and wiping at my teary eyes when I hear one of my sisters thundering down the stairs. I realise as the kitchen door bursts open and bounces back against the wall that it's Leonie. She's been doing that her whole life.

'That was Mum on the phone,' she says as she opens the fridge.

'Don't eat anything!'

'I'm not going to, I'm just looking!'

I scrape the onions from the chopping board into the pan before turning to Leonie. 'And?'

'And what?'

She's eating a chunk of cheese. I knew it. 'And what did Mum want?'

'Oh, right. She's going to be late. She said not to wait for her for dinner.'

I sigh. Mum's been working so much more since Dad died, which I do understand – we lost his wage and even though Mum always earned more, this house isn't cheap to run – but we're going to Italy tomorrow; I thought she'd get home in time for us to have dinner together and get an early night before the flight.

Leonie nods towards the stove. 'How long's this going to be?'

I look round at it, as if that's going to tell me. 'Twenty minutes?'

"Kay,' she says and then opens the fridge for more cheese before going back upstairs.

While the rice cooks, I tidy round the kitchen a bit and then look through the 'important papers' drawer for our passports. I find Mum's and Leonie's, but the next one I find is Dad's. The corner's cut off from where Mum had to send it away after he died. She must have put it back in the drawer when they returned it. It's a terrible picture of him, but I love it because it reminds me so much of going on holiday and him making jokes about how awful the photo was. I remember one time he said he looked like a Beatle and when Mum

7

asked 'Ringo?' he said, 'No, an actual beetle' and then did antennas with his fingers.

I laugh out loud picturing it and it's only when I do a massive snotty sniff I realise I'm also crying.

I put the chilli and rice in bowls in the middle of the table and set three places before shouting up the stairs to tell my sisters dinner is ready. I sit down where I've always sat – far side of the table on the left, the seat that used to be next to Dad – and dish out my own chilli and rice. Leonie and Elyse still haven't come down. I get up, go to the bottom of the stairs and shout them again.

'Just a minute!' Leonie yells back.

'I'm on the phone!' Elyse calls.

I sit back at the table and start on my own food, glancing up at the clock to see how long before Mum might realistically be home. She used to get back from lates by ten, but not any more.

I'm halfway through my dinner and scrolling through Tumblr on my phone when Leonie comes in, flops some food on her plate and heads for the door.

'Where are you going?'

She doesn't even turn round. 'Hmm?'

'Sit down and eat with me!'

'I'm watching Netflix,' she says, half-turning. 'Come up with me.'

'I don't want to come up with you,' I tell her. 'I want us to eat together.'

She rolls her eyes. 'Elyse isn't even here.'

'She will be.'

'Well, call me when she is,' my sister says. And leaves.

I keep eating, but my throat feels tight. It's not that big a deal, I know. And we'll be eating together in Italy. And it's not the same when Mum's not here anyway. But still.

Elyse doesn't come down at all. I put her share in a Tupperware box in the fridge.

Mum doesn't get back until almost eleven. Elyse, Leonie and I are flopped around the living room. We've pulled the cushions off the sofa, watching *Friends* repeats, eating toast and ignoring each other.

'Oh, you're still up,' she says, leaning against the wall in the doorway. She looks tired. She always looks tired these days.

'We were just about to go to bed,' Leonie says. 'We've got to be up at half-five.'

'I know we have!' Mum snaps.

Leonie looks at me and I see the hurt in her eyes before she looks back at Mum and says, 'All right, no need to bite my head off.'

'Sorry,' Mum says. She pushes her glasses up on top of her head and rubs one eye, before saying, 'Shit.' And then, 'Sorry, girls. Forgot I had make-up on.'

'Come and sit down,' Elyse says, standing up and putting a couple of the cushions back onto the sofa.

'No, I'm going to go up to bed,' Mum says.

'There's still some toast,' Leonie says. 'It's not totally cold.'

'I don't want toast,' Mum says. 'I just want my bed.'

The three of us look at each other and then Elyse says, 'It's just . . . we've hardly seen you.'

Mum frowns and then her face seems to crumple a little, but she says, 'We're going to be together all the time in Italy.'

'With everyone else, though,' I say. 'It won't just be us.'

She nods then. She's not looking at me and I don't think she's looking at Leonie or Elyse either. She seems to be looking just past us and I know where without even turning my head. She's looking at the corner of the room where Dad used to sit.

'Okay,' she says, almost to herself. She crosses the room and sits on the cushions Elyse has just picked up. 'So. What have you girls been doing?'

'Milly made turkey chilli,' Leonie says. 'It wasn't entirely gross.'

Mum smiles.

'I found the passports,' I say.

'Oh good,' Mum says. 'I hadn't even thought about that.'

'I've put everything in The Folder,' I tell her and I see her flinch.

The Folder was Dad's thing. All the paperwork for holidays went in there, in order of how we'd use it. So there'd be the confirmation of the airport parking, then the flight tickets, car hire, hotel details, etc. And then the insurance information and European Health Insurance cards would be at the back. He was constantly checking it in the run-up to any trip away and then while we were away, receipts and confirmations went straight into The Folder. And then once we were home, he'd go through The Folder again, chucking stuff out or pinning tickets up on our bulletin board. It was only when The Folder was empty that we really felt like the holiday was over. And all holiday planning began with The Folder.

'Thank you,' she says. 'For doing that.'

'Of course,' I say. I mean, I don't even know how she thought we'd travel without The Folder. None of us ever has.

'I can't wait to get to Italy,' Leonie says. She picks up the plate of toast and puts it on the table next to where Mum's sitting. Mum immediately picks up a piece and starts nibbling.

'I actually need to talk to you about that,' Mum says.

I immediately feel like I'm about to cry. It's not even so much what she says, but the defeated way she says it. It makes me want to curl up in a ball and put my hands over my ears, the way I used to when I was little and didn't want to go somewhere or do something.

'How would you feel about flying out without me,' Mum says.

It's actually not as bad as I was expecting. I was half thinking she was going to say the trip was off. But still. We've never flown without her. And we've all been looking forward to getting away as a family. Even if we're not the family we used to be.

'Why?' Elyse asks.

'I've just . . .' Mum starts to say, but then she puts down the piece of toast she's been eating and picks up a different one. 'I've just got so much to do at work. It's not a great time for me to go away.'

'But you have to come,' Leonie says. 'It's your sister's wedding!'

'Oh, I'm still going to come!' Mum says and she actually looks directly at Leonie, before looking back down again. 'I just don't think I can come tomorrow.'

'No,' Leonie says. I can see red patches on her cheeks and I know she's about to either shout or cry. 'No. Work can wait.

Someone else can cover for you. You have people to cover for you, I know you do. We're going tomorrow. All of us.'

'Leonie,' Mum says in a warning tone. 'My job is important. I don't think you understand –'

'I do understand,' Leonie says, standing up. 'We all understand. We're not babies. We're not idiots. We all understand. But you . . . Since Dad died . . .'

Mum looks up at her then and the pain on her face is so clear that I have to look away. Leonie carries on, but her voice is breaking and I can feel the pain in my throat that I know means I'm about to cry too. 'Since Dad died,' Leonie says again. 'It's like you think work is more important than us. And it's not. It's just fucking not.'

'I know it's not,' Mum says. 'Of course I do.'

'It's like,' Leonie starts as she heads out of the room. 'It's like we don't know how to be a family without Dad.'

As she leaves, Leonie kicks one of the cushions out of the way and I pick it up and put it back on the sofa before sitting down next to Mum. I want to curl into her side the way I did when I was little. I want her to stroke my hair and kiss my head and pretend to bite my fingers. But then I remember it wasn't her who did the pretend finger-biting, it was Dad.

'It hasn't been that bad, has it?' Mum asks.

'It hasn't been that good,' Elyse says.

3

'You've got everything,' Leonie says as I open The Folder and flick through the documents. 'I've seen you check it at least five times already.'

'I know,' I say, pulling out my phone and tapping on the airline's app to double-check the online boarding passes. 'It just feels weird not having much stuff printed out. I mean, what if my phone broke?'

'It's more likely to break with you checking it every two minutes,' Elyse says. 'It's all fine. If anything happened to your phone, I could access the app on mine. Stop worrying.'

I stare out of the taxi window, but it's early and still dark and there's no one on the street. I look at the back of Mum's head – she's in the front with the driver – and think she must be asleep because she hasn't said a word since we got in the car. Actually, she didn't even say much before we got in the car. Just drank some coffee and grabbed her bag and followed the three of us outside when the taxi arrived.

I open The Folder again and Leonie nudges me. 'Give it a rest, Mil. You're stressing me out.'

I close The Folder, but run over its contents in my head again instead.

We check in with no problems. I was worried about the weight of our bags, particularly Leonie's, but it's fine, and then head to security. We have to stand for a couple of minutes while Leonie drinks the rest of the bottle of water she's brought with her, so she can throw it in the recycling, and then we head for the gates.

'Boarding passes?' Mum says, turning to me.

'They're on my phone,' I tell her, taking it out of my pocket for what feels like the fiftieth time this morning.

I tap on my boarding card, hold it over the scanner and pass through the gates. But then I'm on the far side with my phone and everyone else's boarding cards.

'Um,' I say.

'Pass the phone back over and one of you scan everyone else through,' a guard tells me. I pass my phone to Mum, feeling a flicker of anxiety in case she drops it.

Mum tries to scan the boarding card but nothing happens.

'Give it to –' I start to say, but then realise I can't do anything because I'm on the wrong side of the barrier.

'I can't . . .' Mum says. 'It's not . . .'

'You need to scroll it!' I say. 'That'll still be mine.'

Mum pokes at my phone and the urge to reach over and grab it is so strong.

'Scroll it!' I say.

'I'm trying,' she says, through her teeth.

The security guy reaches over and takes the phone and

14

scrolls before letting the three of them through and then giving the phone to Mum.

'Give it to me,' I say, almost snatching it out of her hand.

'Jeez,' Leonie says. 'You really should've had a coffee before we left the house.'

I shake my head. 'Sorry. I just . . . it's not hard.'

'It's fine,' Leonie says. 'We're on the other side. Now you get to pull the stick out of your ass and relax.'

But first we have to go through the security check, which I've always hated. I feel guilty even though I know I've done nothing wrong. When I can see my bag on the scanner I always expect to see the X-ray of a gun or a shitload of cocaine. I hold my breath as I walk through and then pick up my bag, put my shoes back on and breathe a sigh of relief.

'Where are we going to have breakfast?' Leonie asks, once we're all through.

'That place looks nice,' Elyse says, pointing at a cafe, half open to the departures lounge, with white subway-tile walls and pale wood tables.

'Oh, I don't know,' Mum says, looking across at the Starbucks. 'I don't want anything to eat, just a coffee.'

'I'm pretty sure they do coffee,' Elyse says, pointing at the blackboard menu.

'Do they do takeaway?' Mum says. 'I think we probably need to be at the gate.'

'We've got plenty of time,' Leonie says, looking up at the flight information screen. 'The gate hasn't even been announced yet.'

Mum nods and follows the three of us into the cafe. We sit down under a huge mirror, Elyse and Mum with their backs to it, Leonie and I opposite.

'I'm having a full English,' Elyse says, holding up the huge white menu. 'I'm starved.'

I'm not at all hungry, but know that if I don't eat anything I'll be hungry on the flight. I scan the menu, but nothing appeals.

'I might just have a pastry,' I say. 'I'll go and order. Then I can have a look. Mum? Do you know what you want?'

'Just a cappuccino,' she says. 'No chocolate.'

'I'll come with,' Leonie says.

We shove our chairs back and I take a menu with me.

'I don't want anything,' Leonie says, as we stand in front of the chiller, looking at the various fancy juices.

'You have to get something,' I tell her. 'Get a chocolate croissant. Or a pain au raisin.'

'Did you sleep okay?' she asks me.

I frown. 'It took me a while to go off, but then I did, yeah. Did you not?'

'I don't think I slept at all,' she says. 'I'm just going to get a massive coffee.'

'And a banana,' I say, picking one out of a basket on the top shelf of the chiller.

She smiles. 'Okay, Mum.'

'Go and talk to her,' I say. 'I'll sort this out.'

'She's quiet, right?' Leonie says, dipping her head. 'Was I too horrible last night?'

I shake my head. 'I think it needed to be said.'

She grabs my arm, her fingers digging in, and she suddenly looks really young. 'Do you? Because I wasn't sure if it was just me. I mean –'

'What can I get you?' the woman behind the counter asks. I order for Mum and Elyse and I get toast for myself.

While we're waiting for the coffees, Leonie says, 'I'm going to go and apologise.'

'You want to wait for me?' I ask her.

She shakes her head. 'I'm a big girl.'

I grin at her. 'You're really not.'

By the time I get to the table with a tray of coffees, spoons and sugar sachets, Mum and Leonie are looking a bit pink and Elyse is looking at her phone.

I sit down. 'Is everything okay?'

'I'm sorry,' Mum says. 'I'm sorry I've been a bit –'

'It's fine,' I say, shaking my head and passing everyone their coffees. 'Can we just forget about it?'

Mum nods, pressing her lips together. 'But if you ever want to talk . . .'

'Yes,' I say, picking up a sachet and shaking it so the sugar gathers at one end. 'I will. I promise. It's fine.'

She stares at me, nibbling on her lips, so I know what she's going to say before she says it.

'Did you post your acceptance?'

I look down at my coffee and then back up at Mum. 'Yes.'

'You did?' she says, her eyebrows shooting up.

I nod.

'When?' Leonie says.

17

'Last night.' I say. 'While you were painting your toenails and eating all the cheese.'

'That's fantastic,' Elyse says. 'Well done.'

'I'm so proud of you!' Leonie says, flinging both arms around me and squeezing me so hard that I feel something crack in my neck.

'It doesn't mean I'm definitely going,' I say.

'Of course not,' Elyse says. 'You can change your mind at any time.' She's taking the piss, but I decide to let her get away with it.

'This is so wonderful, Milly,' Mum says and she looks almost tearful. 'He would've been so proud of you.'

I nod, swallowing around the lump in my throat.

'Ugh,' Elyse says. 'Enough of this. Can we just get into Holiday Mode now?'

Holiday Mode was another of Dad's things – once we were at the airport, we had to forget all our problems and responsibilities at home and focus on enjoying our time in Italy.

'Sounds like a plan,' I say.

As I stir my latte, I look up at the mirror behind Mum's head. I look tired and pale, but that's not surprising for this time in the morning. And then I notice something I hadn't seen when we first sat down: at the bottom of the mirror are the words 'Pack up! Leave your troubles behind. Let's fly away.'

I think about the acceptance letter, not posted at all, but packed in a zipped pocket in my suitcase and I think, chance would be a fine thing.

* * *

Mum sleeps for most of the flight, while Elyse, Leonie and I read magazines, eat the in-flight meals (out of boredom rather than hunger) and talk about the wedding. Our Aunt Alice was married before, when she was pretty young. She and her husband had our cousin Toby and then split up when he was only a few months old. Toby still sees his dad every now and then, but I don't think anyone else in the family ever does.

Alice and Stefano have been together for years, but they didn't decide to get married until recently. It's been mainly a long-distance relationship too – Alice didn't want to take Toby out of school and Stefano runs the family restaurant in Rome, so there's been a lot of back and forth and Toby working there in the holidays. They moved out there permanently the year before last, after Toby did his GCSEs. Stefano had proposed loads of times over the years, but Alice only accepted after they'd been living together for a while.

'I still don't know why they're bothering to get married,' Leonie says. 'But I'm glad they are. I love a wedding.'

'I think it's nice,' Elyse says. 'They want to commit to each other. In front of everyone.'

'But they were already committed,' Leonie says. 'Alice and Toby gave everything up and moved to Rome. That's pretty committed.'

'Yeah,' Elyse says. 'I guess . . .' She turns a page of the copy of *Elle* she's flicking through and says, 'Me and Robbie are thinking of getting a place together.'

Leonie and I stare at her and eventually, after she's turned at least ten pages, she looks up at us. 'What?'

19

'You and Robbie?' I ask.

'Moving in together?' Leonie adds.

Elyse smiles. 'Yeah. What's wrong with that? It's about time I left home, Robbie needs somewhere to live, we get on great, we can share the bills . . . I mean, it wouldn't just be us, we'd have to have flatmates – but there's this guy at college –'

'Elyse,' Leonie interrupts, putting her hand on Elyse's arm, 'I don't think Robbie will like it when you bring other boys home . . .'

I laugh, but Elyse frowns and shakes her head. 'You're funny. But there are no other boys.'

'Really?' I say. I'm shocked. Elyse has generally had at least two boys on the go for years. She doesn't go out with them both at the same time, but she always seems to have one lined up in case things don't work out with the one she's with. She's always liked to keep her options open, flirt, nothing serious. The thought of Elyse settling down is, well, insane.

'I can't imagine you settling down with just one boy,' I say.

'It's not "settling down"!' Elyse says, flinging her long hair back over her shoulder. 'We're not, like, getting a mortgage or a family car or a dog or anything. It's just more like a flat share.'

'Yes,' Leonie says. 'But it's still a commitment.'

Elyse shrugs. 'Maybe that's okay.'

'God,' I say.

'What about you?' Elyse asks Leonie. 'No boys you like?'

'Nah,' Leonie says. 'All the boys I meet are total dicks.'

'Sometimes that's good,' Elyse says, grinning.

'Ew,' Leonie says, with a straight face.

They both go back to reading their magazines and I realise that neither of them asked me.

'Er, hello?' I say when I realise they're not joking, they've just ended the conversation.

'Hello,' Leonie says, resting her head on my shoulder.

I shrug her off. 'How come neither of you asked me?' I pull my elbow in as a steward rattles past with a trolley.

'Asked you what?' Elyse says, looking genuinely confused.

'If there's anyone I like!'

'Oh, for fuck's sake,' Elyse says. 'First of all, I know there isn't, because if there was you would have said. Secondly, you haven't been out for months, so unless you've totally changed your preferences and got off with someone at school it seems very unlikely. And third, we both – we all – know you're going to be mooning after Luke as soon as we get to Rome.'

'God,' I say. 'I didn't realise I was so transparent.'

Leonie laughs so loud that I hear another passenger tut. 'You're totally transparent. You're like . . .' She screws up her nose while she tries to think of something transparent. 'Cling film?' she eventually says. 'But not so clingy.' She puts her head back on my shoulder.

'Yeah,' I say. 'You're the clingy one. Knobhead. And I won't be mooning over Luke. He's got a girlfriend anyway.'

'How do you know that?' Leonie says. 'Been doing some Facebook stalkin'?'

'No.' I mean, I have, obviously. 'But he had a girlfriend last time I saw him.'

'Which was – what? – a year ago?' Elyse says. 'Come on, Milly.'

'It doesn't matter anyway,' I say.

21

I feel Leonie laugh against my shoulder. 'Sure, Jan.'

I spend the rest of the journey wondering if my sisters are right. They're right that I haven't been out since Dad died. I can't remember the last time. My friends stopped inviting me to things months ago and they don't even bother telling me about them any more. I just see the photos on Facebook. Occasionally I feel left out, but mostly I'm relieved not to have to get dressed up and go and pretend to have fun and be interested in some random friend of whatever boy my best friend Jules fancies. Actually, I don't even think I can call Jules my best friend any more – we barely even speak outside of school and not even in school much either. My sisters have always been my best friends really.

They're wrong about Luke though. There's no way I'm going to waste my time in Rome chasing after him. Not that I would chase after him. But I'm not going to waste my time wondering whether he likes me. Or whether he's with some other girl. Or whether he'd be interested in me if he's not. And I'm absolutely not going to think about what happened after Dad's funeral.

Luke's hot, there's no way around that. He's always been hot. And I'll probably always have a crush on him. But Rome is about family and Aunt Alice's wedding, and food and wine and sun. It's not about Luke. At all.

4

When the captain announces we're landing, Mum wakes up, stretches, smiles and then suddenly looks a bit confused.

'Everyone okay?' she asks us across the aisle.

Frowning, she pulls her hair out of the ponytail it's been in since she came home from work last night. The band has actually left a bit of a ring around her hair, even after she's run her hands through it.

'We're fine,' Elyse says. 'You okay? I can't believe you slept the whole way.'

'I haven't been sleeping very well,' she says, leaning forward to look out of the window as we land.

I pull everything out of the pocket on the back of the seat in front to make sure I haven't left anything. Leonie snatches the magazine out of my hand and starts flicking through it, as I put the other bits back in and then check my phone in my pocket.

'Did they say what the weather was going to be like?' Leonie asks. 'I missed it.'

'Hot,' Elyse says, tipping her head back and closing her eyes, ready for landing.

'Good,' Mum says and closes her eyes too.

I lean forward and look out of the window as the ground comes closer and closer and then brace myself for the bump as we land.

Stefano's arranged for a car to pick us up from the airport. But we all stand outside for a few moments, just feeling the sun on our faces.

'It smells different here,' Leonie says, pulling her sunglasses out of her bag.

'That's jet fuel,' Elyse says.

'Pfft,' Leonie says. She actually says 'pfft'. 'It's Italy.'

'It's good to be back,' Mum says quietly, her sunglasses hiding her eyes.

And it is. We first came when we were all small. I don't remember anything about it except that it was really hot and Leonie whinged about it the whole time. Since then we've come almost every year. We used to stay in the hotel Dad had worked in, but since Alice met Stefano we've stayed at San Georgio. At least a week every summer, longer if Mum could get off work. Which she used to. Sometimes. But not any more.

In the car, Elyse texts and Mum closes her eyes again, but Leonie and I stare out of the windows. The first half of the journey is just motorway, but once we get to the outskirts of Rome, I start to feel excitement bubbling up inside. Leonie points out pizzerias and gelaterias, while I stare at the pink and peach and cream and terracotta buildings and think about Dad. I can't believe he's not here with us. I can hear him talking about the history, making up stupid facts about different buildings and stories about people sitting outside cafes or screaming past us on mopeds.

It's ridiculous, I know, but I almost feel like he's going to be here. He'll be waiting for us at San Georgio. He'll have flowers for Mum because he knows she'll be annoyed that he tricked us, but we'll be so happy to see him that we'll all grab him and hug him and the flowers will get ruined.

I know it's not going to happen. I know he's gone. But part of me just can't believe it. How can it be real that I'm never going to see him again?

I hadn't realised I was crying until Leonie reaches out and wipes a tear off my cheek with her finger – and then she licks it.

'Oh my god,' I say. 'You are gross.'

Leonie just shrugs and then rests her head on my shoulder again. I rub my face against the top of her head. She's totally disgusting, but I love her so much.

The closer we get to the square, the tighter the roads get. I can never actually believe that cars can go down some of the streets they go down in Rome. There are cars and mopeds parked on both sides, along with tourists wandering around without looking. The streets leading to Campo de' Fiori are cobbled and it's the feeling of the car rattling over the cobbles that really brings it home to me that we're in Rome. And in just a few minutes we're going to see Alice and Toby and Stefano.

And Luke. I feel sick.

We pass our favourite gelateria – Leonie got totally addicted to their cherry meringue flavour last time we were here – and

25

she presses her face up to the car window, making puppyish whimpering noises.

The driver stops in front of the flower stalls at the end of the square and we all clamber out of the car, waiting as he gets our luggage out of the boot. I start to look around the square, but I have to stop. It's too overwhelming. It's busy and noisy, but it's just so Rome – which is so Dad – that missing him physically hurts. My stomach feels hollow and empty and I want to curl up and cry. I feel someone's arms wrap around me from behind and then Elyse says, 'I miss him too,' into my ear.

I let out a sob and she squeezes me. Leonie presses up against my side. I look at Mum, but she's got her arms wrapped around herself and the expression on her face makes my heart hurt. Then Alice is directly in front of us, flinging herself at Mum, and I can see a blurry Stefano through my tears and I wipe my face and let him hug me hello.

For a few minutes it's all just hugging and kissing and giggling. I always forget how absolutely gorgeous Stefano is: big brown eyes, wavy brown hair, stubble, lovely lips and the accent, of course. It takes some getting used to. Plus he smells amazing, like smoke and basil and oregano. But he squeezes me and kisses the top of my head and laughs with Mum and Alice and by the time we're inside the restaurant I've stopped thinking about it. Mostly. (He really is very gorgeous.)

The terrace in front of the restaurant is crammed with tourists, bowls of olives and glasses of beer on the table in front of them. We go inside through the side door and it takes my eyes a few seconds to adjust to the relative darkness. It's much cooler inside and much less busy. The locals – people we've seen here ever year, but never really spoken to – are standing at the bar with their coffees. They nod and smile at us and I see a man reach out to pinch Leonie's cheek, but she yanks her head out of the way. I laugh. She wouldn't have done that last year; he would've pinched her and she would've complained about it for the rest of the day. I hear her mutter 'Back off, grandad,' as we walk on and Mum must hear her too because she gives her a sharp look.

The restaurant is always exactly the same: bare brick walls, arched mirrors that look like windows, strings of white lights on the ceiling and red tablecloths on the round tables, white napkins folded into the wine glasses. At the far end of the room, the kitchen is open and bright with chrome and non-atmospheric lighting, but it's empty right now.

We follow Alice and Stefano right through the restaurant and out to the back garden, which is where they're getting married. Unlike the restaurant itself, the garden has changed a bit since we were here last year. The terrace with its white wrought-iron seating now has a pergola over the top, which is covered with vines, bunches of purple flowers tumbling down, throwing the tables into shade.

'Sit down,' Stefano tells Mum and Alice. 'I'll get us drinks. Are you hungry?' he asks and then shakes his head. 'I'll just bring food.'

'We're fine,' Mum says, but we all know she doesn't mean it. Stefano's food is amazing. None of us would dream of turning it down, whether we were hungry or not.

Mum and Alice sit at the table on the edge of the garden.

'Toby's out there,' Alice tells me, Leonie and Elyse, so we head down the two steps into the main garden area.

The willow trees in the corners of the garden have grown so much that the garden seems much more private. The highest wall is covered with a climbing plant dotted with huge white flowers and just in front of it is a stone fountain that wasn't there last year.

But the most important thing is at the far end: our cousin Toby, lying on his back in a patch of bright sunshine, his hands behind his head and feet crossed at the ankles.

'Sorry to disturb you, dickhead,' Leonie says, dropping down to the ground next to him and immediately digging her fingers into his waist to tickle him. He's always been ridiculously ticklish.

'Piss off,' he says, slapping her hands away, but then he sits up and gets her into a headlock. 'Bloody hell, Leonie,' he says, pushing her away from him. 'You look like a girl again!'

Last year, Leonie had her hair cropped just before we went to Italy. It was very short and Toby took the piss out of her the entire time. Now her hair is chin length and actually suits her much better.

Elyse and I sit down on the grass too and Toby beams at us both. 'It's so good to see you!'

'You too,' I say, smiling at Leonie, who is trying to fix her hair where Toby scuffed his hands through it.

'Where's Luke?' Elyse asks. And I tell myself to remember to slap her for it later.

'Just coming now,' Toby says, gesturing behind us.

I want to turn around, but I can't. I won't. I look down at the grass and focus on a single blade, longer than the rest. I tuck my hands under my thighs and feel the grass pricking the backs of my fingers.

'Hey,' Luke says, dropping to the ground next to Toby.

'Stefano sent these,' he says, holding up a cardboard carton of Coke in bottles. I think he's even taller than last year – or maybe he's thinner? His hair is still long; it's tucked back behind his ears, but it's probably as long as mine, almost to his shoulders. And he's still beautiful. Cheekbones and dark blue eyes and full pink lips.

'They're cold,' he says. 'Just got them out of the fridge.'

'Thanks,' Elyse says, taking one.

My hands are still under my thighs and I'm starting to think about wriggling them out, when Luke holds a bottle out towards me. I pull one hand out from under my leg and reach to take the bottle from him, focussing on a droplet of condensation rolling down the outside of the glass, rather than looking at Luke. Some Coke bubbles over the top of the bottle and runs down the back of my hand.

'Oops,' I say without thinking, tipping my hand to let it run off.

'Hi,' Luke says, his voice low.

I force myself to meet his eyes and I feel that flip in my stomach again. The flip I always feel – have always felt – when Luke looks at me. He smiles and his smile is still the same too: slow and sexy and the flip in my stomach moves lower.

I pull my eyes away from Luke and focus on Toby. He asks us about the journey and we ask him about working in the restaurant – how busy it's been, how much they get to go out, the wedding preparations. And then he's off, telling us hilarious stories about dresses and food and music and the new stone fountain Alice wanted and Stefano couldn't get right, and I listen to him and think about the first time I ever saw Luke.

It was in Aunt Alice's garden in her house in London, before she and Toby had moved out to be with Stefano full-time. It was one of those summers when it seemed to be golden and warm and beautiful every day and Alice started having barbecues almost every evening. Neighbours and friends and family would just drop in, bringing burgers and sausages and beer and wine – and Luke was there with Toby.

I saw him as soon as we walked out through the French doors and onto the raised decking. He was down on the grass, standing in front of the impromptu goal Toby had set up with a couple of folding chairs and a yard brush. He was wearing white football shorts, a black T-shirt and white socks. His trainers were on the decking, just in front of where I was standing. Even though he and Toby were just in socks, they were having a kickabout while everyone else either stood around the edges of the garden or up on the decking where the barbecue and the drinks were.

Toby and Luke had been friends for years. Luke had been at school with Toby but then his parents split up and he and his Mum moved out of London, but Luke seemed to spend most weekends round at Aunt Alice's with Toby. For a while I wondered if they were a couple and I hated that I hated the idea of it because I wanted Toby to be happy. But I wanted Luke more.

Dad was there; he joined in for a bit, messing about and showing off rather than playing seriously. I liked how Luke joined in the messing around with Dad. Sometimes if parents get involved in something like that, people roll their eyes or act like they're embarrassed, but Luke and Toby just treated Dad like one of the lads. Before too long, other men had joined in and then some little kids and it was chaos.

I remember noticing Mum watching Dad and she looked so proud. I knew how much she loved him. He must have noticed her too because when he scored a goal – a completely ridiculous one that bounced off the shed door and knocked over a plant pot – he ran over and picked her up and twirled her round. Later on, just as it was getting dark, the solar lights hanging in the trees and dotted around the edge of the lawn glowing white, Alice put some music on and Dad sang along, pretending to use the barbecue tongs as a microphone. He didn't need a microphone – his voice was more than a match for the acoustics of Alice's garden.

'Milly,' Elyse says, bumping me with her shoulder.

'Sorry, what?'

'Are you okay?' Elyse says. 'I thought you'd gone into a trance.'

'Sorry,' I say again. 'I was just thinking about something and I spaced out.'

'Obviously,' Leonie says, laughing.

'Sorry. I'm tired,' I say, glancing at Luke.

'Why don't you go up to your room?' Toby says. 'Get settled in and then have some food when you come down later.'

'Yeah,' I say. 'Yeah, I think I will. Thanks.'

I tip my head back and squint up at the bright blue sky. A couple of seagulls squawk overhead. I always forget there are seagulls in Rome.

31

'I'm staying here,' Leonie says. 'In the sunshine!' She lies back down on the grass, closing her eyes.

'I'm going to stay for a bit too,' Elyse says. 'Is that okay?'

'Oh, I'll stay as well then,' I say, looking at my sisters.

'Oh, god, go,' Elyse says. 'We're only going to be in the garden, we won't go anywhere without you.'

'No, I'll –' I start to say.

'Go,' Leonie says. 'We'll stay here. Promise.'

I nod. I really do want to go and have a lie down. 'Okay.'

I stand up and brush at my leggings in case there's grass sticking to them. Leonie lies back down and says, 'See you later.'

On the terrace, Alice and Stefano fret over me a bit too – Mum's in the bathroom, apparently – but I tell them I'm fine, just tired, and manage to extricate myself and go up to my room. Elyse is sharing a room with Mum and I'm sharing with Leonie. We've stayed in this room before, but last time Elyse had to squeeze in with us too – because Dad was with Mum – so there's a lot more space this time. I close the huge window that looks out over the square, and the room is suddenly so quiet that I open the window again to test the difference. Window open: shouting, laughter, music, mopeds revving; window closed: dead silence.

I close the internal shutters, plunging the room into darkness, kick off my shoes and lie down on top of the quilt, staring up at the ceiling where a line of yellow light shines from the space at the top of the shutters. I suddenly don't feel as tired any more, and I know immediately that I won't fall asleep. I put on the bedside light and pick up my bag, rummaging in the internal pockets until I find the tiny pot with Dad's ashes.

I'd been worried that they might set alarms off at the airport, but they didn't, thank god. I run my fingers over the top of the pot and then lie back down, holding it in my hand.

Since I know I'm not going to sleep, I should probably go back downstairs and join everyone else, but I don't. I stay in my room. I stay and think about Dad. And Luke. At Alice's barbecue.

By the time Dad started singing I was sitting on the wooden steps, feeling a bit woozy from the heat and the one glass of wine Mum had allowed me to have, but feeling really lucky and happy. Elyse was going out with a boy called Rio at the time – he was leaning on the fence and she was leaning back against him with his arms around her waist. Leonie was sitting on the grass cuddling a little white dog someone had brought along. Luke came over and sat down next to me. He felt warm. Even though he didn't touch me at all, I could feel the heat coming off him. He said, 'Your dad's really cool.' And I laughed. It was the perfect thing to say, obviously. I think I managed to squeak out something like 'He's all right, yeah.' And then we just sat there, listening to Dad singing.

I wish I could remember what song he sang. I should ask Elyse or Leonie. Or Mum or Alice. It's the only detail I really don't remember. When whatever song it was finished, Luke stood up and as he did his leg brushed against mine. I was wearing a dress and it was like getting an electric shock. He glanced back over his shoulder, grinned and said, 'See you later.' And then Dad called me to go up and sing with him. I shook my head – I didn't even trust my legs to get me up off the steps and across the garden – and then someone changed the CD and people started dancing and the moment was gone.

I lie there in my huge bed in Rome for a while before I give up and cross the room to look out of the window and down at the square. But all I can think of is Dad standing down there, looking up at me, singing that stupid Cornetto song.

I spend the next hour or so lying on my bed and reading a book on my phone until my eyes start to get hot. I put my phone to one side and I've just closed my eyes to try to nap again, when Leonie bursts in. She throws herself on the bed next to me and I bounce on the mattress.

'Wake up, sleepyhead,' she says, her mouth right next to my ear.

'I haven't even been to sleep,' I say into the pillow. 'I literally just closed my eyes. Why are you such a pain in the arse?'

'You love me,' she says.

'Unfortunately,' I say. I roll over and scoot myself back against the padded headboard and squeeze the satin quilt in my hands.

'So what've you been doing?' she says. 'Wanking?' She gets up and opens the internal shutters, flooding the room with light.

'Oh my GOD, Leonie!' I say, squeezing my eyes shut.

'Not my fault you're repressed,' she says. 'I thought that's what you'd come up here for. Saw Luke again, looking all hot and holding those Coke bottles with the water dribbling down them all seductively . . .' She looks at me under her eyelashes and pouts. 'I thought you were overwhelmed with lust.'

'Stop talking now.'

'Seriously though,' Leonie says, swinging around the bed so her head is dangling upside-down off the side. 'He's ridiculously sexy. And he likes you.'

I roll my eyes. 'He doesn't.'

She frowns. 'He does. I bet you . . . something I've got that you want.'

'You haven't got anything I want,' I say, smiling.

'No? Natural charm? Black toenails? Perfect pitch?' She grins at me.

'You haven't got perfect pitch,' I say. 'I've got perfect pitch.'

'Oh, yeah,' she says, lying back down. 'I forgot. It's been so long since I've heard you sing.'

Not that again. 'I'm going for a shower. You lie there and think about something you can bet me.'

'Oh yeah,' she says. 'A shower . . .' And then she does an over-the-top wink.

I throw my pillow at her.

When I come out of the bathroom, wrapped in one of the amazing fluffy cotton robes Alice bought for every room, Leonie has got the window open and she's leaning out. The room is a mess – Leonie's literally just upended her bag on her bed. I pick up one of her dresses and hang it up in the wardrobe.

'Stop tidying,' Leonie says, without looking around. 'Come and look.'

I go and stand next to her at the window and look out. The square is crammed with market stalls, selling everything from cheese and vegetables to baseball caps and handbags. Little half-van cars are buzzing around and getting held up by the pedestrians. There's obviously a pizza stall somewhere down there because I can smell garlic and roasted tomato and someone's singing an Italian song I don't recognise – it might be a busker or it could easily just be one of the stallholders. The air is warm and I take a deep breath.

'Could you live here?' Leonie asks me.

I shake my head. 'No. I don't think so. It's too different.'

'The first time we came – remember? – you said you never wanted to leave.'

I look at her. She's still looking down at the square.

'There's a difference between saying you never want to leave somewhere when you're on holiday and actually really wanting to live there full-time. I like home.'

'I do too. But I'd like an adventure.'

I laugh. 'The idea of you on an adventure scares me.'

'Maybe that's what I should bet you. If Luke likes you, you'll agree to have an adventure with me.' She turns from the window and grins at me, pushing her long fringe out of her eyes.

'I'd need to know a lot more about the adventure before I'd agree to that.'

She threads her arm through mine and rests her head on my shoulder. 'I'll think of something.'

5

By the time Leonie and I meet Mum and Elyse downstairs in the bar, the dinner service is in full swing. Italians eat late, and take a long time over their meals, so the earlier service is mainly tourists. Since we had a late lunch, we're going for a walk first and then coming back to eat after the rush is over. Mum and Elyse have both got glasses of wine and so Leonie and I get a Coke between us while they finish.

'Did you sleep this afternoon?' I ask Mum.

She nods. 'A little. Feel better for it though. Did you?'

I shake my head. 'I just read.'

'Or something,' Leonie says and I give her the finger, quickly. Not quick enough though.

'Milly . . .' Mum warns.

'Sorry.'

Leonie sticks her tongue out at me.

'You look lovely,' Leonie tells Mum.

And she does. She's more dressed up than I've seen her for a while, in baggy white trousers, a black top and sparkly sandals — plus, she's wearing make-up and she's put her hair up. She always has her hair up in a bun or a ponytail for work, but she's done it in a nice piled-up style with bits falling down.

'Thanks,' Mum smiles. 'You too. Apart from the T-shirt.'

It's an Iron Maiden Eddie T-shirt Leonie found in a charity shop and cut up so it's cropped and sleeveless. It's her favourite.

'Where are we going to go?' Elyse asks without looking up from her phone.

'Has Robbie called?' Leonie says, in an annoying swoony voice.

Elyse swats at her. 'He's texted, yes.'

'Missing you?'

Elyse smiles. 'Of course.'

'And are you missing him?' I ask her.

Elyse actually gets a soppy look on her face. 'I am, actually. More than I expected.'

'That's nice,' Mum says. 'I like him.'

I notice Elyse's eyebrows flicker in annoyance, but I'm not really sure why. It's good that Mum likes Robbie, surely? Unless Elyse is thinking if Mum likes him he must be too nice. She's done that before, when she went through the whole bad-boy-the-parents-won't-approve-of phase, but I thought she was past that.

Elyse drains her wine, stands up, smoothing her shirt-dress down over her hips and says, 'Are we ready?'

'Oh, I don't think I'm going to come,' Mum says.

The three of us – Elyse, Leonie and me – all stare at her, but she's looking out towards the garden.

'Why not?' Elyse says.

Mum glances up without actually properly looking at any of us and then says, 'I said I'd help Alice out with some wedding stuff. You three go, though. Have a good time.'

The *passeggiata* is an Italian evening tradition. It's a stroll before dinner, I suppose is the simplest explanation. The first time we came and we saw people just walking around, we kept asking Mum and Dad where everyone was going, but they weren't going anywhere, they were just walking and chatting and hanging out. Some of the older people sit outside restaurants and bars drinking and chatting; people stop and join in the conversations, children run about and any babies get passed around. And the Italians get quite dressed up for it. I absolutely love it. It's so much nicer than coming home from school or work and flopping out in front of the TV. Although at home, that's all I ever seem to have the energy to do. It's different here. I feel different here.

'Alice is working,' Leonie says, once we're out on the square.

The market is closing – men are taking down and packing up the stalls, a street-sweeping van, driven by a woman, I notice, is turning in circles around the statue in the middle of the square. On one side of the steps to the statue, a woman is playing an accordion and on the other side, a group of teenagers seem to be setting a small fire while laughing hysterically.

'That doesn't mean she couldn't be doing something for her,' I say.

We dodge out of the way of a small boy who is throwing a tiny blue and purple light-up helicopter toy into the air and catching it again, and head towards Leonie's favourite gelato shop.

'She just didn't want to come with us,' Elyse says.

There's a huge queue at the gelateria, so we turn down one of the side streets. Fairy lights loop from one side to the other. There's a mix of shops, from tourist gifts to designer clothes, to shops selling sausages and cheese – and at the end, the street opens out into a small square, on one side of which is a beautiful white building. The top of it is sort of shaped like a cello – big curves and then smaller curves – and I can hear Dad's voice in my head describing the architecture. Not that we ever really took any of it in, but I loved hearing him talk about it.

Rome is so amazing for this. The most normal looking little streets – streets lined with mopeds and with washing strung between the buildings – and then the most incredible ancient and beautiful buildings. Dad had a name for it.

'What did Dad used to call this?' I blurt out.

'What?' Leonie says.

'The beautiful buildings in the middle of normal streets?'

'Oh!' She frowns. 'I can't remember.'

'I can't either,' Elyse says. 'I'm not even sure it was a real word. I think he made it up.'

'Like "nuzzery",' I say and we all laugh.

Dad told us that when you drive down a road and the trees on either side have met in the middle to form an arch, it's called a nuzzery. We were all impressed with him for knowing it, I think, and I'm sure we all used it at some time or another. And then one day we were talking about it and he admitted he'd made it up. He didn't even admit it, actually – he thought we all knew.

'I used that stupid word in an essay,' Leonie says and we all laugh again.

'I miss him so much,' Elyse says, sitting down on the steps.

'I can feel him here,' Leonie says.

I sit next to Elyse and dig my fingers into the cool stone underneath my thighs and Leonie drops down on my other side and rests her head on my shoulder.

We sit there for a while watching the people outside the bar opposite. There are two men having what looks like a heated argument, but is probably just a standard passionate Italian conversation. I think about how Dad would have been over there, chatting, buying drinks and getting drinks bought for him, speaking bad Italian, laughing and making everyone laugh. Dad was the person everyone was waiting for when you went out – or even stayed in. He was the one who got everything going, who made everything fun.

I know what Leonie means about feeling him here, though. He loved Rome. He originally came when he had a year out and he and Mum stayed the whole time, working in a hotel. Dad sang there in the evenings. It was his place. And I can just imagine him walking around a corner to join us. It's harder to imagine that he won't.

I used to be able to imagine it at home too. As I walked towards the kitchen or the living room, I'd picture him sitting there and I could do it so well that I'd really expect him to be there. Sometimes I thought I could smell him. But then I'd open the door on an empty room and it was just like a punch in the stomach. I couldn't stop doing it. It was like I was rehearsing him being alive again, the same way I used to rehearse him being dead. And then when he did die, I learned that rehearsing it hadn't helped at all.

'We should get back,' Elyse says, standing and reaching her hands back to pull Leonie and me up too. We walk back a different way and on the next street we approach a doorway where a couple are pressed up against the wall, kissing enthusiastically. He's mouthing at her neck and she has her head tipped back, resting against the wall. Her eyes are closed, long eyelashes fanned out over her cheeks, and her red lips are parted. He's got one hand pushed under her strappy white top. I can see his knuckles pushing out the fabric, his hand moving slowly, and I feel a pulse between my legs. And then he lifts his head from her neck and I realise it's Luke.

My feet stutter on the pavement and Leonie links her arm with mine and sort of hugs me against her.

'Keep walking,' she says, her voice low, her mouth close to my ear.

I keep walking, but I'm breathing so quickly I'm surprised Luke and the girl don't hear it. Or feel it. I feel like I'm vibrating with embarrassment and shame. Again.

6

'Did you see Luke?' Stefano asks, when we're barely through the door. 'He should have been back from his break ten minutes ago.'

I feel my face flame, but Leonie cuddles me again and says, 'Let's go upstairs for a minute.'

'We passed him on the way back,' Elyse tells Stefano.

Stefano rolls his eyes. 'Was he with his girl? Always sneaking out for . . .' He makes a kissing noise.

'Come on,' Leonie says, pulling at my arm.

I let myself be steered out of the restaurant and up the stairs to our room. Leonie shuts the door behind us and I drop face-down on my bed. I feel Leonie's hand rubbing circles into my back.

'Fuck,' I say into the quilt.

'Oh wow,' Leonie says. 'It must be bad if you're dropping F-bombs.'

I turn my head to one side so she'll hear me more clearly. 'Fuck off.'

She drops down next to me, face close to mine, eyes wide. 'It doesn't mean she's his girlfriend.'

'Stefano said she was,' I mumble.

Leonie wrinkles her nose. 'Stefano probably just mean a girl. A girl he kisses.'

'Please don't remind me,' I say, turning my face into the quilt again.

'Did you think he'd been waiting for you?' Leonie says gently.

'Ugh.' I roll onto my back. 'Of course not. But I just . . . I hoped that he maybe wasn't seeing anyone. Okay? I know it's embarrassing.'

It's not as embarrassing as what I'd really hoped for, but I'm not telling Leonie that.

'That's not embarrassing,' Leonie says. 'That's perfectly reasonable. You like him. You've liked him for a long time. And he likes you too –'

'Yeah,' I say, rolling onto my side again. 'Looked like it.'

'Oh, come on,' Leonie says. 'You've kissed other boys. Since you met Luke. You and Jake –'

'I don't want to talk about Jake.'

'I know. You never want to talk about Jake. Or Jules. Or the band.' She blows out a breath. 'You kissed that boy at that party –'

'Oh my god!' I say, shoving at her shoulder. 'I did not kiss him. He kissed me. And grabbed my boob. And stuck his tongue halfway down my throat. And blew smoke in my face.'

'And that doesn't work for you?' Leonie says, grinning. 'I just mean . . . Just because Luke was kissing someone else, doesn't mean he doesn't like you.'

'He's always kissing someone else,' I mumble.

Leonie doesn't take me seriously. Instead she sits up and says, 'Yes, darling, he's always kissing someone else. All the time. Literally never see him without a girl stuck to his face. Next time it could be you!'

'Yeah,' I say. 'Dream big.'

'Get up. Wash your face. Put on some red lipstick. Go downstairs and make him regret every minute of his life he has spent not kissing you.'

I sit up. 'I'll wash my face.'

'That's a start,' Leonie says.

She waits outside the bathroom while I splash cold water on my face, put on lipstick – pink, not red – and blot most of it off again.

'There you go!' she says when I come out, as if she's talking to a child. 'Much better.'

I do feel better. Not much. But a bit.

Leonie grabs my hand and pulls me towards the door. 'I tell you one thing we've learned tonight,' she says, as we step out onto the landing. 'That Luke knows his way around a tit.'

Even though the restaurant is theoretically closed now, there are still plenty of stragglers. A few people have stayed to have a pre-wedding drink with Stefano and Alice, but it's still a lot calmer than when we left earlier. It's such a warm, fun place, I'm not surprised people find it hard to leave.

My stomach flutters with nerves at the idea of seeing Luke, but I keep my eyes straight ahead and tell myself Leonie's right. Him kissing someone doesn't change a single thing: nothing was going to happen between us anyway.

45

Alice waves us through to the garden where a large table is already groaning under the amount of food piled on it. Gia, one of the waitresses, is setting the table around it and Leonie immediately goes over to help.

'Stefano says you must all start to eat,' Gia says. 'No waiting for the rest to be ready.'

Me, Mum and Elyse sit down and Gia says, 'I'll just go and get some wine.'

'Are you joining us, Giancarla?' Mum asks.

Gia smiles. 'Is that okay? Stefano said I could . . .'

'Of course,' Mum says.

Gia had just started working here when we came last year. We didn't get to know her very well, but she seems nice enough.

'She goes by Gia,' Leonie reminds Mum, as Gia goes inside for the wine.

I tip my head back and close my eyes – they're gritty with tiredness. When I open them I see that there's a full moon. Hazy clouds are just drifting away and there's a blueish glow around it.

'Look.' I point up.

Mum and my sisters look and Mum says, '*La Luna*. Want to wish on it?'

We all close our eyes. I think about wishing for Luke to like me. To want me. For me to somehow be the kind of person who can work out how to be with him. But instead I wish for Mum to be happy again. I don't know, but I bet Elyse and Leonie are wishing for the same. I can't begin to imagine what Mum's wishing for.

46

* * *

Toby's the first to come out and join us and, unlike me, he's not embarrassed to start on the food.

'Go on!' he says, shoving what look like deep-fried mozzarella balls into his mouth. 'Dig in. You know Stefano won't be impressed if you don't.'

I pile some bruschetta and prosciutto onto my plate and then Gia appears with the wine and a few bottles of water.

'I'm under instructions not to go back in there,' she says, smiling. 'They shouldn't be too long – they're saying goodbye to a couple of jokers who can't stop wishing them "*in bocca al lupo*".'

I look at her blankly.

'It means "in the mouth of the wolf" for, you know, good luck.' She smiles at me. 'It's not serious.'

I've just stuck a chunk of bread in my mouth when Luke comes out. He stands at the head of the table and asks, 'Anyone need anything?'

I shake my head – my mouth's too full to speak – and then wipe some oil off my chin.

'Great,' Luke says, sitting down. 'Cos I'm knackered.'

'I bet,' Leonie whispers to me and I elbow her.

'Busy night?' Elyse asks. I'd elbow her too, but she's on the other side of the table and I can't reach.

Luke nods. He's already pouring himself a glass of wine.

'It's always busy,' Toby says. 'But tonight was a bit crazy. Everyone's so excited about the wedding.'

'It's going to be amazing,' Elyse says.

47

'It had better be,' Alice says, coming out from the restaurant, carrying yet more food: pasta, fish and a plate of something in batter. 'It's put years on me,' she says.

Mum smiles at her. 'Don't give me that, you've loved every minute of it! And you look beautiful.'

Alice does a little curtsey and then flops down onto a chair. 'Well, thank you. But I feel about a hundred.'

Mum's right, she does look beautiful. She looks a bit like Mum but where Mum's tall and fair, Alice is shorter and darker. Mum doesn't really tan either, but Alice seems to go brown as soon as she gets to Italy. When we were little she had the longest hair I'd ever seen – she could almost sit on it – but it's been getting shorter and shorter over the years and now it's in a kind of pixieish bob and it really suits her, shows off her cheekbones.

Eventually Stefano comes outside. He looks his usual gorgeous self, despite the fact that he's literally been slaving over a hot stove for hours. He sits down, pours himself a glass of wine and tops up everyone else's glasses, including mine, then says, 'To family. And to friends.'

We all clink glasses and as I sip my wine, I notice Luke is looking at me. One of his eyebrows flickers up and then he smiles at me. I smile back, ignoring the flip in my stomach.

'And I just wanted to say,' Stefano says, 'while it's just us, before everything goes completely crazy . . .' He holds his glass up towards the moon and for a second I think I see the moonlight reflected in his glass. 'Dominic, you are very much missed.'

My throat is too tight to speak, but some of the others say, 'To Dominic.'

I want to look at my sisters, Mum, my family, but I can't make myself do it. I stare down at my plate until the food blurs in front of my eyes.

He's not here. He'll never be here again. And nothing's ever going to be the same.

7

'You awake?' Leonie says.

'Mmmmm.' I stretch my toes to the end of the bed and reach my arms up over my head.

'These beds are freakishly comfy,' she says. 'I haven't slept that well for ages.'

After Dad died Leonie used to come into my room and get in bed with me in the middle of the night. At first it woke me up, but after a while I didn't even know she'd done it until I woke up in the morning squeezed up against the wall with her knees or her elbows digging into me. We never really talked about it and then she just stopped.

There's a knock on the door and then it opens slightly. 'Are you two awake?' Elyse whispers.

'No,' Leonie says at the same time as I say, 'Come in.'

'Did you have the best night's sleep ever?' Leonie says, kicking off her duvet and stretching her pyjama-clad legs up to the ceiling.

'Not really, no,' Elyse says. 'Mum was crying in her sleep.'

I sit up. 'Really?'

Elyse nods.

'Did she wake up at all?' Leonie asks.

'No,' Elyse says. 'It was really weird. At first I thought she was awake and so I tried to talk to her, but then I realised she was still asleep. She did it on and off all through the night. At least it seemed like that. I don't feel like I've had much sleep, anyway.'

'God,' I say, my voice cracking. I swallow hard. I don't want to cry. But the thought of Mum keeping it together when she's awake and crying in her sleep . . .

'Should we talk to her?' Leonie says and without looking I can tell she's crying.

'I don't know,' Elyse says. 'I don't know what to do for the best. How are we meant to know what to do?'

I wipe at my eyes and try to slow my breathing down. 'I think if she wanted to talk about it, to us, she would do. Maybe she's just not ready yet.'

Leonie sniffs and presses her foot against my leg. 'Maybe.'

'Is she asleep now?' I ask Elyse.

'I think so. She was asleep when I left.'

'Maybe it's a good thing,' Leonie says, her voice still small. 'Maybe she's been in denial all this time and now . . .'

It makes sense, I suppose. Mum's been pushing it away and now it's finally hit her.

'I guess that's healthy?' I say.

'I think so,' Elyse says.

'Fuck. Poor Mum,' Leonie says.

We sit in silence for a bit, and then my sisters convince me to go downstairs to get hot chocolate for the three of us.

'You can see what Luke looks like first thing in the morning,' Elyse says. 'Maybe he's really hideous.'

'I doubt he's even up,' I say, but I brush my hair and put on mascara and lipgloss just in case. Like an idiot.

When I get downstairs, Toby's in the kitchen singing along with the radio. Or rather, howling along with it since it's an Italian song and he clearly doesn't know the words.

'Did you sleep well?' he asks as he pours hot water into a teapot.

'Tea?' I ask.

'Yeah, for Mum. Stefano's tried to convince her to start the day with coffee, but he's not having any luck.'

'You're taking them breakfast in bed?'

Toby shudders. 'God, no. Stefano's already gone to the mark –' He stops and says, 'Hey, man.'

I get that clenched, fluttery feeling in my stomach again and I turn and see Luke walk in. He is in no way hideous. He's clearly come straight downstairs from bed. His hair is all over the place and I think he's even got pillow creases on his face. He's rubbing his stubbly chin with one hand and he pushes his other hand back through his hair. He's got a fairly fresh-looking burn on the back of his wrist. I want to touch it.

'Morning,' he says, his voice rough and croaky. It makes my stomach twist.

'I slept like the dead,' he says, taking a step towards the coffee machine. He stops. 'Oh shit, Milly. I'm sorry.'

He's got the little frown line between his eyes and he looks mortified.

'No,' I say. 'Don't worry about it. Honestly.'

'No, that was totally tactless.' He reaches out and touches my arm and my skin prickles.

'It's fine, really,' I say, tightening my fingers on the countertop I'm holding onto.

I look at Toby and see him look from Luke to me. I narrow my eyes at him and he holds his hands up and grins.

'What's your order?' he asks me.

I don't know what he means at first, but then I realise. 'Oh. Hot chocolate. Three, please.'

'What about Aunt Carrie?'

'She's sleeping in,' I say. At least, I hope she is.

'So, what's happening today?' Luke asks.

He pulls a chair out from under the breakfast bar and leans against it rather than actually sitting down. I can see the muscles in his forearms, the prominent bones in his wrists, his knuckles, his long fingers curled around the back of the chair. I imagine how they'd feel inside me and have to look away, my face heating up.

'Setting up the garden,' Toby says. 'A day of hard labour ahead.'

'I'd better go and get a shower then,' Luke says and as he straightens up, I get a glimpse of a strip of tanned skin just under the hem of his T-shirt and it takes my breath away. I always thought that was an exaggeration, but I do actually feel a catch in my chest and I have to concentrate on my breathing.

Toby switches the coffee machine on to add the hot milk to the hot chocolate and once it's finished its noisy whooshing and hissing, he laughs and says, 'God, you've got it bad.'

'What?'

He turns and grins. 'Luke. You lurve him.'

'Oh my god, Toby!' My face is burning. 'Is it obvious?'

The phone rings and he puts one finger up to tell me to wait, and goes through to answer.

I can't believe I've made – or am still making – an arse of myself over Luke again. After the last time. And after I said I wasn't going to. This is why I'm not interested in relationships. I don't understand how it's all supposed to work. Elyse tells me it's easy: you like someone, they like you, you flirt a bit, you arrange to go out. It's like that song Dad used to sing about us. That's all about how easy love is. Like taking candy from a baby, apparently. Although I don't think that's so easy either. But I just don't see it. All that happens to me is I get a crush on someone, they turn out not to be interested or to have a girlfriend or I manage to spectacularly fuck it up, like I did with Jake.

'He's not seeing anyone, you know?' Toby says, walking back into the kitchen.

'Luke?' I say, stupidly.

'No, the Pope. The Vatican's closed for the wedding,' he says sarcastically. 'Yes, Luke.'

'What happened to that girl . . . back at home?'

Toby scrunches his face up. 'Was it Melissa?'

'No.' I sigh. 'Hannah.'

'Ah yes. That didn't last very long at all. Maybe a couple of days after the . . . you know, funeral.'

I want to lean over and just bang my head on the table, but I restrain myself.

'What's the problem?' Toby says. 'You clearly like him, he likes you, you're both all right to look at, neither of you is a dick . . . I mean, he has his moments, but –'

'You think he likes me?' I ask without lifting my head.

'Of course he likes you. What's not to like?'

I take a deep breath and figure I'll just come out with it. 'Did he ever tell you what happened after the funeral? At your house?'

He frowns. 'I don't think so, no. Why? What happened?'

I shake my head. 'It doesn't matter.'

'Something happened between the two of you, you mean?'

I lift my head and look up at the ceiling. There's a partially deflated balloon nestled in the corner.

'I . . . yeah. I mean . . .' I think about telling him. I think about telling him exactly what happened. But I can't do it. 'Sort of. It wasn't a big deal. It was just . . . a thing.'

'Did you kiss?' he says, grinning.

I shake my head. 'We saw him. Last night. He was round the corner, feeling up some girl in a doorway.'

'Long blonde hair?' Toby says and then holds his hands out in front of himself to suggest big boobs.

'Ugh,' I say, swatting at his hands. 'But yes. Exactly.'

'I bet that was Carolina.' Italian pronunciation: Caro*lee*na. 'There's nothing going on there.'

I roll my eyes. 'He had his hands all over her . . .' I hold my hands out in front, same as Toby had.

Toby pulls a face. 'Well, yeah. I mean . . . not *nothing*. But he's not into her.'

'He looked like he was into her.'

'I think they hook up sometimes, yeah, but she's not, like, a girlfriend or anything.'

'Do you do that?' I say. 'Just hook up? Kiss some random girl, give them a thorough breast exam, go on with your life.'

'I don't, no,' Toby says.

'No, cos you're nice.'

'I'm delightful. But Luke's good too. He just sees girls sometimes. He gets given a lot of numbers. And sometimes he calls them. There's nothing wrong with that.'

'Right,' I say. 'That doesn't really make me feel better.'

Toby puts the three cups of hot chocolate on a tray.

'He likes you,' he says, shrugging. 'That's all I know.'

I scratch at the countertop with a fingernail. 'I just . . . I don't want to be Toby's cousin who happened to be in Rome.'

'I don't think you would be. He's a good guy, Mil. For reals.'

I nod. 'Okay.'

'You'd better take that upstairs before it goes cold,' he says, nodding at the tray.

8

Once everyone's showered and dressed, Alice calls a meeting. She tells me, Leonie, Elyse and Mum to go out for the day.

'There must be something we can do,' Mum says.

'You don't understand, Carrie,' Stefano says. 'Alice has organised it all like the military. Every moment is accounted for. If you are standing in the wrong place at the wrong time someone may thread flowers into you –'

'Or turn you into a hog roast,' Toby says, grinning.

Alice playfully swats at them both. 'Seriously,' she says. 'You need to go and relax. Have a lovely day. In a couple of days there'll be relatives to entertain and you'll be on the go all the time. This is meant to be a holiday for you all. Go sightseeing. Or just go and sunbathe somewhere. Just go.'

'Will you three be okay?' Mum says, putting a bottle of water in her bag. 'You'll stick together?'

'Or you could come with us,' I say. 'Or maybe we could go with you for a bit?'

'I do not need to see another Caravaggio,' Leonie says, rolling her eyes at me. 'When are we going to Dad's hotel?'

I look at Elyse and find Elyse is looking at Mum, who is looking at Leonie.

'I don't . . .' Mum starts. 'I didn't think that we . . .'

I hadn't thought that we would either. I can't even bear to think about going without Dad.

'We have to!' Leonie says, looking from Mum to Elyse to me. 'It's a tradition. We can't not!'

'It was a tradition with Dad,' Elyse says.

Not even that. It was Dad's tradition first. It just became our tradition too as we got older. Whenever we came to Rome, we'd go back to the hotel Dad had worked at and have a drink in the bar. When Mum and Dad first came, most of the people Dad worked with were still there, but over the years, almost everyone has left. Last time we went – last year – there were only two people still there and one of them was about to leave.

'What do you think, Milly?' Mum asks me and for a second I feel like I can't breathe. She hasn't asked me anything. For ages. And now she's asking me this? I shake my head.

'I don't think . . .' I say quietly. 'It won't be the same.'

'Of course it won't be the same,' Leonie says. She sounds upset and I shield my eyes to look at her again. She's looking at Mum. 'It's never going to be the same again! We know that. But we shouldn't just . . . stop. We have to . . . We're still here. We're here, in Rome. And we're still a family and –'

'Okay,' Mum says. 'Okay.' She stands up and walks back inside.

I hear Leonie gulping to catch her breath. My hands are shaking.

'You didn't have to do that,' Elyse says, after a couple of minutes.

'I did,' Leonie says. 'I know it's going to be hard. I'm not stupid. But it's bad enough being here without him. If we didn't go . . . it'd be like we'd forgotten him.'

I shake my head without looking up. 'It's not,' I say. 'But it's too hard. Maybe next year.'

'But what if we don't come back next year?' Leonie says. 'This could be the last time.'

'It's not going to be the last time,' I tell her. 'I wish you'd stop saying that!'

'But it could be, Mil,' she says gently. 'You should probably accept it.'

I shake my head. I won't accept that. I don't want to accept that.

'It'll be fine,' Elyse says. 'Don't worry.'

We're all quiet for a moment then because we know all too well that no matter how much you worry, something terrible can still happen completely out of the blue.

Elyse, Leonie and I don't really have an idea of what we want to do and so at first we just wander around the flower market. I post some photos to Instagram and we cross the square, sniffing at some sprigs of lavender one of the stallholders gave us.

'Is there anywhere you really want to go?' Leonie asks me, snapping most of the stem off her lavender and tucking the flower behind her ear. I thread mine through the strap of my top. Elyse just drops hers in her bag.

'I was thinking the Trevi Fountain, maybe?' I say.

We walk to the end of the side road and stop on the corner of the main road, in front of a bridal shop.

'God, that's beautiful, look,' Elyse says, pointing at a short, clingy dress with a flowing cape attached.

'Are you seriously looking at wedding dresses?' I ask.

Elyse pulls a face at me. 'For fashion reasons.'

'Better be,' I say.

She puts her hand on her heart. 'I can promise you now I'm not planning to marry Robbie.'

'No,' Leonie says, stepping to the edge of the kerb to look for a taxi. 'Just move in with him.'

'Yes,' Elyse says. 'What's wrong with that? It makes sense, doesn't it?'

'It makes more sense to stay at home,' I say.

'It makes more *financial* sense to stay at home,' Elyse says, tugging Leonie back from the edge of the kerb as a bus rumbles past. 'But I'm twenty. I can't stay at home for ever. I want to live somewhere I can have friends round, have parties, not have my little sisters texting me in panic if I'm not home by midnight . . .'

'That happened once,' I say, my skin prickling with remembered embarrassment.

Elyse drops her arm around me and squeezes me against her. 'I know. And I get it, I do. I just . . . I want a bit more freedom.'

Leonie waves madly and a taxi heading in the other direction does a U-turn and stops directly in front of us.

The driver can't get us all the way to the fountain because the streets are too busy with cars, so he drops us and says, 'Down there,' pointing ahead. But when we get to the end of the street, we don't know where we are.

Elyse pulls her phone out to check on the map, but Leonie yanks it out of her hand.

'We're obviously not far away,' she says. 'I'm sure we can find it ourselves.'

'But what's the point, when I can just look it up?' Elyse says, reaching for her phone just as Leonie shoves it into her bra.

'If you think I won't go into your bra for it –'

'Come on,' I say, as a moped swerves around us. 'Let's just walk.'

We've only taken a few steps when Leonie says, 'Trevi Fountain?' to an Italian woman standing outside a shop.

The woman points the way we're heading and then pinches Leonie's cheek and says, 'Bella.'

We keep walking. Leonie flitting from shop to shop, looking at posters of the movie *Roman Holiday*, tiny metal Coloseums, decorations made of brightly coloured glass balls.

'Just give it me back for a minute,' Elyse says, as we reach the end of the street and we're still not at the fountain. 'I just need to send one text and then you can keep it for the rest of the day.'

'Like I'm going to fall for that,' Leonie says.

'Cross my heart,' Elyse says, drawing an X on her chest with her index finger.

'One. Text,' Leonie says, pulling Elyse's phone out of her bra and handing it over.

'Ew. Warm,' Elyse says, looking around and then walking a few steps away to sit on a bollard outside a shop.

'Do you think they really will move in together?' I ask Leonie, as we turn a postcard carousel outside a shop a few doors down.

Leonie pinches my cheek. 'You are so naive, it's adorable.'

'Oh, shut up. I won't be patronised by my baby sister. I just . . . I can't imagine them living together. It just seems so . . .'

'I really don't think you need to worry about it,' Leonie says. 'You know what she's like. She's never been with one boy for longer than five minutes until now. And whenever we came here with Mum and Dad she practically pulled in the airport.

'Okay, done,' Elyse says, joining us. 'No more texting today. Fuck him.'

'Oh, to be in love!' Leonie jokes, grinning. 'See!' she mouths at me.

'Shut it,' Elyse says.

'Phone,' Leonie says, holding her hand out.

Elyse holds the phone out as if she's going to give it to her, but then shoves it into her own bra.

'Oh, hell no,' Leonie says and pounces on Elyse, trying to get her hand into her bra.

Tourists tut as they walk past us, my sisters grappling and laughing, but then Leonie manages to get the phone and sticks it back in her own bra.

'You crossed your heart, Elyse,' she says. 'You don't fuck with that, you monster.'

Elyse laughs, shoving her so hard she staggers and almost bumps into some people walking past.

'Sorry! Sorry!' Leonie says.

At the next crossroads, Leonie gestures at a newsstand on the corner. She buys some chewing gum and asks the man the way to Trevi Fountain. He rattles off directions in fast Italian and Leonie beams at him and thanks him.

'Did you understand any of that?' I ask her, as we wait to cross the road.

'This way,' she says and grins at me.

'Ever get the feeling that taxi driver was taking the piss?' Elyse says.

'You've changed,' I tell Leonie, ignoring Elyse.

'Me?' Leonie says. 'How?'

'You're so much more confident.'

'Because she was such a wallflower before,' Elyse says, sarcastically.

'No, she wasn't,' I say. 'But she's different now.'

'I love it when you talk about me like I'm not here,' Leonie says.

We cross the road and stop for a moment to look up at an amazing pink and white building – it's like a turret without a castle.

'I do feel more confident,' Leonie continues. 'It's really weird. I just feel like I can be myself more.'

'Because Dad died, though?'

'I don't know. That's weird, right?' She stops and looks at me for a second and then we keep walking. 'I know I could be myself with Dad, I never worried about that at all, honestly. Actually, I think I was probably more concerned about what Mum would think. But then after Dad . . . I just feel more grown up. Is that stupid?'

'No, it's not stupid at all,' I say. 'But it's the opposite of how I feel.'

'I know,' Leonie says. 'We worry about you a lot.'

'I know you do. It'll be okay, I think. I hope. I just feel . . . I sort of feel lost without him, you know?'

My eyes fill up and when I look at Leonie I see hers have too. Elyse drops her arm around my shoulder.

'I miss him so much,' Elyse says. 'But I think I just want to be better for him. I want him to be so proud of me.'

'I want to make him proud too,' I say.

'I know,' Leonie says. She squeezes my arm. 'You will. Just wait till you get to Liverpool.'

The Trevi Fountain is unsurprisingly busy, it being a Sunday. The wall around the fountain and the steps are all crammed with people, taking photographs and trailing their hands in the water. We squeeze through – past a couple kissing dramatically in front of the fountain, and a toddler, wearing reins and eating a gelato while sobbing loudly – and get down the steps to the fountain itself. We sit on the edge and Leonie holds up her phone and says, 'Selfie!'

'Oh, so it's fine for you to have your phone?' Elyse says.

'I'm not as addicted as you,' Leonie says. 'And I'm not wasting my time in Rome sending photos of shit flats to my boyfriend.'

Leonie takes her selfie. Elyse starts laughing.

'What?' I ask her.

'Remember when Dad's sunglasses fell off?' she says.

I start to laugh too. 'God, yeah. I'd forgotten about that.'

'I think I've still got a photo on my phone,' Leonie says, scrolling at her screen.

I turn around as Leonie scrolls through her photos. The water looks turquoise, but it's clean and clear and I can see hundreds of coins glinting on the bottom.

'Here!' Leonie says.

The photo shows Dad leaning over the little wall we're sitting on, his arm in the water, fingers stretched out for his sunglasses that are just beyond his reach, other arm braced against the wall. He's laughing so much his eyes are almost closed, mouth open. It's so perfectly Dad that I laugh out loud just looking at it and then immediately start to cry.

'How can he be gone?' I say. 'I know I keep saying this, but . . . how?'

'I know,' Elyse says, cuddling me against her again.

'Sorry,' Leonie says from my other side. 'I didn't mean to make you cry.' She kisses my shoulder.

'No,' I say. 'It's good. It's a good photo. And I'd forgotten.'

I look up, wiping my face with my hands, and see rows of people in front of me, some laughing, others taking pictures, the people at the top eating gelato. One woman gives me a sad smile and I smile wetly back at her.

'I was going to sprinkle Dad's ashes here,' I say.

Leonie says, 'Really? Like . . . now?'

I nod. 'They're in my bag. I've had this image in my head of me sitting on the edge and trailing the pot through the water. Stupidly didn't even think about how many people would be here.'

'You can still do it, can't you?' Elyse says. 'Who's going to stop you? There's no sign saying "no sprinkling ashes".'

'"No bombing, no heavy petting, no dead fathers",' Leonie adds.

I pull a face. 'You two are sick in the head.' I lean against Elyse.

'Dad wouldn't have minded,' Leonie says, leaning against my other side. 'He would have thought it was funny too. The three of us with our little pots, not knowing what to do with him.'

'You don't know what to do with yours either?' I ask her. Leonie's had her pot on her bedside table at home and I just assumed she found it comforting. I thought I was the only one who had conflicted feelings about it.

'Do you know where Mum's is?' I ask.

Elyse shakes her head. 'Mine's in my bedside drawer, so maybe hers is too?'

'I've never seen it,' Leonie says.

'I know dipping my finger in it is weird,' Elyse says.

Leonie snorts.

'I just . . . I opened it because I wanted to see what it looked like. And then I just sort of thought "that's Dad". That's all I've got of him. So I know it's kind of gross and creepy, but . . . it's still Dad. Does that make sense?' Elyse says. 'Or are you squicked out?'

'I mean, I don't think I would want to do it,' Leonie says. 'But if it makes you feel better, I think it's fine.'

'If I think of it as him I feel better, but then I think, well, it's a little pot of ashes . . . because he's dead. Then I feel worse,' Elyse says. 'And I wonder if I'd feel better if I didn't have it. And I could think of him as he was and not as he is now. Or *isn't* now, I suppose.'

'That's how I feel,' I say. 'I've been feeling guilty – shouldn't I want to hold on to this last bit of him?'

'Or maybe you just want to let him go?' Elyse says. 'And move on?'

'I don't want to let go of memories or anything, but I do think I could let go of the . . . pot,' I say.

'I like the idea of him swimming around in the Trevi Fountain,' Leonie grins. 'Not that he would be, but . . . you know.'

'I know. That's what I was thinking,' I say. 'That he'd like a bit of him to be in Rome.'

'We should sprinkle a bit in all his favourite places,' Elyse suggests.

'Foyles. The history department,' I say.

'The cheese counter in Morrisons,' Leonie says.

'The Draper's,' Elyse says. 'On karaoke night.'

'The Apple Store,' Leonie says, punching the air as if that's Dad's ultimate resting place.

I burst out laughing. 'Oh, we should throw the whole lot in there.'

'I don't know,' Elyse says. 'I think if you thought of the Trevi Fountain, that's where you should do it.'

I nod. 'I was thinking that too. And I really don't want to get a lifetime ban from the Apple Store.'

'Isn't it going to make a mess?' I ask Leonie.

She's still standing and looking up at the fountain. 'I'd forgotten how noisy it is,' she says.

I look up at the rushing water too then. She's right, it's not quiet.

'I think you're right,' Elyse says. 'It'll make like a big grey cloud, won't it?'

'And everyone will see. And I'll probably get arrested.'

'Not to overdramatise or anything,' she says, smiling.

'I don't know,' I say. 'It just seems wrong.' I dangle my fingers in the cool, clear water. 'It's not like it was in my head. I don't think I can do it.'

'No,' Leonie says. She rummages in her bag and then hands me two Euros, passing another two to Elyse. 'We could still throw coins in though, eh?'

'Absolutely,' I say, smiling.

Elyse just drops hers in, looking down into the water. I turn my back on the fountain and throw one coin over each shoulder.

'Two for a new romance!' says Leonie.

9

As we're crossing Campo de' Fiori towards San Georgio, Leonie hooks her arm through mine and pulls me against her.

'Look at the sky!'

I look up. It's bright blue, the sun so dazzling it hurts my eyes.

'Ow,' I say, shoving at her. 'Thanks for that.'

'What are those flowers?' she says. 'The big pink ones?'

She pulls at my arm and I yank myself away. 'Stop being weird! You're hurting me!' I push her away from me and as I do I see Luke. Further down the square, in front of the gelateria. With a girl.

'I was trying not to let you see,' Leonie says, tugging on my arm again.

'No,' I say. 'It's okay.'

He looks gorgeous. As always. Tanned and relaxed and confident and just utterly suited to Rome. I feel sweaty and slightly stressed and my shoe has rubbed the skin off the back of my heel. I need to go inside before he sees me. But I can't seem to look away.

'Is that the same girl?' Elyse asks, squinting from behind her sunglasses.

The girl is standing astride a moped. She's wearing tiny shorts and wedge-heeled sandals and her legs look impossibly long. The vest top she's wearing has a drapey neck and low armholes and I hope she's wearing a bra otherwise she'll be flashing everyone as she drives. Maybe that's what she wants.

Luke laughs, ducking his head – I don't know if I can hear it or if I just know how it sounds – and she reaches out and touches his forearm. Exactly where I noticed the burn earlier. Why didn't I touch it? I wanted to. But I didn't. Why is it so easy for other people to flirt and I just can't make myself do it? She tips her head back to laugh, her hair falling back like a silky curtain.

'Oh, she's good,' Leonie says. 'A+ flirt skills.'

For a moment I think maybe he won't fall for it. Maybe it's too obvious. But then she's stepping off the moped, one long, slim leg swinging over the seat, and Luke's moving round so that he can climb on.

'Can we go in now?' I say, looking down at my hands. I put my thumb to my mouth and gnaw on a hangnail.

'I want to see what happens,' Leonie says. So much for protecting me from the sight.

'It feels weird,' I say. 'Like we're spying on him.'

'We are spying on him,' Elyse says. She holds her phone up in front of my face. 'Would you live here?' The photo is of a tiny studio flat with what looks like a shower cubicle next to the cooker.

'No,' I say instantly.

The girl is climbing onto the moped behind Luke, scooting her hips forward until she's pressed right up against his arse. I feel that throb in my crotch again. I wonder if it does actually turn you on, riding a moped? Surely the vibrations of the road must travel up and –

'I'd have made him get on behind me,' Leonie says. 'It's her bike.'

'Weight distribution,' Elyse says. 'Safer for him to be in front. And now she can fondle him and grind up against him. She's smart.'

I groan. 'Seriously. Why are we still watching this?'

'Cheap thrills?' Elyse says. 'What about this one?'

She shows me a photo of what looks like a garage, but with a sofa and beanbag chair.

'Are you joking?' I say. 'That looks like where you'd keep someone you kidnapped.'

'It might come to that,' Elyse says, half smiling. 'They're all so shit, I just need to find the least shit. And they've all started to blur into one.'

Luke has started the moped now. I can hear the low buzz of the engine. The girl has her arms wrapped around his waist, her chin hooked over his shoulder. He's grinning and they just look so perfect together that it makes me want to throw up.

That night, I can't sleep. I lie for a while listening to Leonie snoring and making this grunting sound she's done since she was a kid – she says it's to itch the inside of her ear and it sounds really weird. I don't mind it though. It means I don't need to check she's still breathing.

71

The room is mostly dark, but every now and then a pattern of lights sweeps across the ceiling from cars passing the square. I think about Luke and the girl on the moped and wonder where they went and what they did when they got there. I reach down and pick up my phone, propping one of my pillows up to shelter Leonie from the light from the screen.

I scroll through Twitter and Instagram, liking stuff randomly, and then click over to Facebook. My friend Jules has posted a few memes, but nothing personal. I click over to her photos, even though I know it's going to hurt.

The top photo is of the band, but it's a selfie: Jake is holding the camera and Jules, Amy and Liv are doing duck faces. I should be there. I should be crouching down at the front, totally failing to do a duck face, as usual. The next photo is a Timehop from two years ago, taken in the cafe in the park after we'd been messing about there all day, playing football, racing each other on a circuit of the play area, just lying around and talking and laughing. It was a good day.

We'd all drawn moustaches on our fingers – I can't remember why now – and in the photo, we're holding them to our top lips. I stare at myself on the photo. Dad was alive then. I was in the band then. We'd been arguing that day about which songs to do if we got to play at this local festival thing Jake was trying to get us into. Jules wanted to do 'Somebody That I Used to Know', but she kept getting wound up cos Jake would sing 'Baa Baa Black Sheep' over it every time. I wanted to sing something by Sia: 'Chandelier' or 'Titanium'. Jake wanted to do 'Mr Brightside'. We argued about it all day, but still couldn't agree.

I remember Jake grabbing my finger and holding it up to his lip, pouting. And how I wanted to touch his mouth when I'd never really thought about it before. How I wanted to grab his moustache finger and put it in my mouth. Right there, in front of everyone. And how I saw his eyes go wide and thought he must've known what I was thinking, must've seen it on my face. And I pretended I was late and had to go. And I left.

Everything was different and I had no idea what was coming. I touch the screen, covering my face with my thumb. I wonder what songs they do now, without me. I wonder if Jules sings everything or if Jake sings sometimes too – he had a nice voice, but he wasn't really confident enough to sing on his own.

I think about posting a status, but all I want to say is 'I miss everyone' so I don't.

I swing my legs out of bed and sit for a second trying to work out whether I'm awake enough to get up or tired enough to try to go back to sleep. Leonie does the grinding thing again, so I get up and slip out of the room, taking Leonie's hoodie that she's left on the floor just inside the door. The stairs are dark, but the lights are on in the restaurant, so I head towards the terrace, pulling Leonie's hoodie on as I go. It smells like her Daisy perfume.

I open one of the double doors to the terrace and jump, letting out an embarrassing squeal, when I see that Luke's already out there.

'Hey,' he says, looking up from his own phone, his hair falling down over his eyes.

'Sorry,' I say, blushing. 'I didn't expect anyone else to be up.'

He's sitting at the last table on the terrace. He's wearing red-and-white checked pyjama bottoms and a white T-shirt and his feet are bare. It's like seeing someone you've had a dream about. Only worse. Because I think about him all the time when I'm awake.

I stand awkwardly in the middle of the terrace, wondering whether I should just go straight back to bed. But Luke looks so good like this, soft and sleepy in the half-dark, that I can't make myself leave.

He pushes a hand back through his hair, but the strands fall straight back down again. 'Couldn't sleep, huh?'

I shake my head. 'You?'

'I've got into this weird habit of waking up at, like, five. And just being wide awake. It's annoying.'

He's fiddling with something on the table and I step closer. 'What's that?'

He holds it up to show me. 'Amaretti biscuit. I made hot chocolate and I couldn't resist. Want some?'

'Oh,' I say. 'No. It's yours.'

'I didn't mean this.' He gestures at the large mug pushed to one side of the table. 'There's more.' He stands up, actually lifting his chair so it doesn't make a scraping sound and says, 'Sit down. I'll get some for you.'

'It's okay,' I say. 'I can just get a glass of water . . .'

'Sit,' he says, lifting the opposite chair away from the table. 'I'll be back in a minute.'

I sit down and wince – the metal is cold on the back of my legs and the tile floor is cold under my feet. I put one foot on top of the other and lean my elbows on the table, looking out into the garden.

It's still night, but I can tell it's on the way to being morning. It's dark, but there's something about the darkness, something hazy, as if it's already drifting away. It's probably no more than half an hour until sunrise. I already know I'm not going back to bed. Dad once told me never to miss a chance to watch a sunrise or a sunset, and I never have. He loved the moon too. I stand up and walk down onto the grass to see if I can see it.

The grass is cold and damp, but feels good under my feet. I turn in a circle, looking up, but the moon isn't visible, even though the sky is clear enough that I can see stars scattered like sugar on a countertop.

'No moon tonight,' Luke says and I jump again.

'God,' I say. 'I'm a nervous wreck. Stars though,' I say, pointing up.

He just smiles at me. 'Do you want this out there?' He's holding another bowl of hot chocolate. I can see tendrils of steam curling up from between his hands.

'No, I'll come back,' I say. But I've only taken a couple of steps when I realise I don't want to. 'Actually, I think I will stay,' I say. I turn and point to the table over in the corner of the garden.

Luke walks over, carrying the hot chocolate and wincing as he steps onto the cold grass.

'Do you know what time it is?' I ask him, as we cross the garden to the table. 'I want to watch the sunrise.'

'It's 5.15,' he says. 'So you shouldn't have long to wait. Won't see much from here though.'

'That's okay,' I tell him, sitting down and realising too late that the chair is wet.

'Careful!' I say, but it's too late for him too. We grin at each other as he slides the hot chocolate across the table to me.

'I just like seeing the sky get brighter,' I tell him, wrapping my cold hands around the bowl.

He nods. 'The start of a new day.'

When who knew what might happen, I think, but don't say.

'Hey,' he says. 'You okay?'

I shake my head. 'Yeah. Sorry. I just thought of something. Something about my dad.'

'You miss him a lot,' Luke says.

I don't look up at him. 'Yeah. I just thought . . . He used to say a new day was like a blank page and you could write whatever you wanted.' I glance up. He's looking straight at me, his face serious. 'But now I think of it differently. When I think "anything could happen" I think of the bad things. I think, like, today could be the day Mum dies too. Leonie could get run over. Elyse could get mugged.' I point back at the restaurant. 'There could be a gas leak and the whole place is gone.'

'Shit,' Luke says. 'Rough day.'

I laugh out loud and then cover my mouth, glancing up at the windows above the garden. 'I know. I know it's ridiculous.'

He smiles. 'It's not. It makes sense. After what happened.'

'Do you do it?' I ask him, leaning forward so the steam from the hot chocolate dampens my skin. 'Do you think of the worst case scenario? For everything?'

He frowns and looks as though he's really thinking about it. 'Sometimes. But I don't really . . . It's hard to describe.' He picks up the biscuit and fiddles with the wrapper. 'I don't really even think about it. It's like a bad thought kind of skids

76

through my mind, but doesn't stop. And I've always been stupidly optimistic. I've always thought everything will work out. I've been told it's annoying.'

I smile, turning the bowl in my hands. 'Thinking the worst is annoying too. Ask my sisters.'

'Leonie's like me, right?' Luke says.

I picture Leonie - her bright face grinning at me, laughing, taking the piss. 'Yeah. And the weird thing is that she's more like that since Dad died. She's more confident. And more positive. And she just . . . she loves life.'

'And you don't?'

'I . . .' I pick up the hot chocolate and blow over the surface, watching the liquid ripple away from me. 'I do. But I'm scared all the time.'

'I think everyone is,' Luke says. 'But they try to hide it.'

'Do you think so? Really?'

'Yeah. I mean . . . My dad, right? He and my mum had me. And everything was great for a while. And then he met someone else. And he left. And they had a kid. And then he left them too. And for a while I thought . . . he just likes the start. The easy part. The falling in love. The excitement of a new life, a new family, a new baby.' He twists the plain silver ring he wears on his middle finger. 'And then he leaves and does it again. But that's because he's shitting himself, you know? The responsibility of it. He doesn't mean to do it, he just gets scared.'

'Do you see him?'

Luke looks up at the sky and then back down at the table. 'Yeah. Not, like, a lot. But he's all right. He got back with the woman he left us for. She's nice. And the baby's great – he's not even a baby any more, he's three. But it's like . . . he used to be my family. He and my mum were the most important people in my world. And now he has this new family and when I go and see them, I'm like a guest. I mean, I am a guest. And we all know it. So it's different.' He shuffles in his seat. 'And then my mum got married again and it's sort of the same at home too. They're a new family. That's why I'm here. I just needed to get away. It's like my family doesn't exist any more.'

I can't speak. I try to blink away the tears that are threatening to spill, but they fall anyway. I wipe them quickly.

'Oh, shit,' Luke says. 'Milly. I'm sorry. That was really fucking tactless. Again. I –'

'No,' I say. 'Don't. It's fine. It's just . . . that's what I keep thinking about. It's hard to think about. That the family that we were is over. And we're never going to be that family again. But it sort of makes me feel better that it's not just us, you know? God, that sounds awful, like I'm glad you're having a shit time too. I don't mean that.'

Luke smiles. 'I know what you mean.'

'I mean . . . this terrible thing happened to us. But terrible things happen all the time and people survive. They go on. It's fine.'

'And it'll get easier,' Luke says. 'I know that sounds like shit and everyone always says it, but it really will.'

'I know. But I'm sort of scared of that too. Like, when it gets easier it's because I don't miss him so much or I start to forget. I don't want to not miss him.'

'I don't think you forget. I think you adjust.'

I stare down at the surface of my hot chocolate and pick at the peeling paint on the metal seat under my thighs.

'Do you think . . .' I glance up at him. 'Maybe that's why Mum's been the way she's been since Dad died.'

Luke just looks at me intently, waiting for me to go on.

'She works all the time. And she doesn't really talk to us any more. We were so close – the five of us, you know?'

'I remember,' he says, quietly.

'And since Dad . . . It's like we lost her too. She works all the time. And it's like she keeps herself from us. Does that make sense?'

'Have you asked her?'

I shake my head. 'We don't really talk about that kind of thing. But I think . . . I've been telling myself it doesn't make sense. That she should want to be with us more now that it's just the four of us, and we're all . . .' I can't think of the right word and my eyes fill again.

'Grieving,' Luke supplies.

I nod and swallow, trying to calm my breathing before speaking again. 'But maybe she's scared. Of doing it all alone. Of losing us.'

'You are,' Luke says, gently. 'So why do you think she wouldn't be?'

I nod and quickly wipe at my eyes. 'I guess because she's an adult. But, I mean, I am too. Theoretically.' I glance at him and see him smiling back at me.

'Theoretically,' he repeats. 'But don't you think everyone's just pretending?'

I laugh. 'I don't know if that's comforting or terrifying.'

'Both?' he says.

I stare at him for a couple of seconds and I want to kiss him. I want to tell him that I've wanted him since the first time I saw him. That I think about him all the time. That it scares me how much I think about him. That I remember the way his hands felt on my skin. That it scares me to think he might not want me, but it scares me even more to think he might.

'Do you want to talk about it?' he says, still looking straight at me. I can only look at his eyes for a second before I have to look away. 'The funeral?'

'God,' I say. I want to stand up and run straight back inside. 'No. I really don't. Is that okay?'

He smiles up at me quickly, before looking back down at the biscuit. 'That's fine. But . . . I just wanted you to know that it was good. I –'

'Please don't,' I say, my face heating.

'Sorry,' he says, glancing up at me again. I look away.

For a few seconds we're both quiet and I can hear one of the street-sweeping vans rumbling through the square. I'm about to get up and go back inside when Luke says, 'Want to see something cool?'

I nod.

'Wait here,' he says, stands up and jogs across the wet grass, back into the restaurant.

I watch him go and then look up at the sky. So many stars, but they won't stay still. As soon as I feel like I've focussed on one, it zooms away, leaving a trail of silver. I can't tell if they're actually shooting stars or if it's my eyes.

I hear the door bang and look up to see Luke crossing the grass towards me.

'Oops,' he says, as he sits down. 'Let the door go.' His mouth pulls to one side and he looks so young and guilty that it makes me laugh.

'Ready for the cool thing?'

I nod. I am. I think.

He unwraps the biscuit and pushes it across the table to me, before smoothing the wrapper out and rolling it into a tube. He stands it up on one end, then strikes a match on one of the San Georgio matchbooks Stefano keeps in a bowl on the counter near the till. He lights the top of the wrapper and it immediately starts to burn down, like a sped-up candle. We both watch as the flame flickers and leaps. Just before it burns out altogether, the wrapper tips over on its side on the table and turns to ash.

'Shit,' Luke says. 'That's not what's meant to happen.'

I laugh. 'No.'

'You've seen it before,' he says.

I nod. 'My dad used to do it.'

'Sorry,' he says. He looks confused. It makes him look younger.

I shake my head. 'That's okay.'

'I don't know why it didn't work,' he says.

'Maybe there's too much breeze? Or not enough?'

'Maybe it's a metaphor,' he says, the corner of his mouth quirking up.

I laugh so suddenly that I actually snort. 'It's not a fucking metaphor!'

81

He grins at me. 'I don't think I've ever heard you swear before.'

'What's the metaphor?' I say. 'It's like life. I thought I could fly, but instead I just fell over sideways.'

'And turned to ash,' Luke adds, poking at the remains of the wrapper.

'Oh, shit,' I say. 'That is a fucking metaphor.'

Luke laughs. 'I knew it!'

I stare at the little pile of ash on the table and wonder if it would be too weird to mention the little pot of my dad's ashes upstairs. I look up at Luke and find he's just staring at me, his eyes serious. There's a small, brown birthmark just above his collarbone that I've never noticed before, and my fingers itch to touch it. I move my right hand out from its position tucked under my leg and flex my fingers to get some feeling back. As I reach across the table, I can see the red ridges where the metal of the chair has pressed into my hand. Or where my hand was pressed into the chair. Luke doesn't move as I reach out until my fingers are just in front of him, when he dips his head, his hair falling forward and brushing the back of my hand.

I hear myself gasp, but I bite down on my lip and keep moving until I'm touching the birthmark. His skin is warm against my cold fingertips and I want to touch him more. Touch more of him.

'Milly,' he says, under his breath, looking up at me.

I want to slide my hand around the back of his neck and lean across the table and press my mouth to his. I still remember how it tastes, although it probably tastes of chocolate right now. I want to push the table out of the way and climb into

82

his lap. Instead, I trail my fingers over his skin before tucking my hand back under my leg.

'Sorry,' I say, looking down at the table.

I hear him sort of huff out a laugh. 'You don't have to say sorry,' he says. 'That was –'

'Morning!'

I look up and my eyes skitter over Luke before looking past him to Toby who is standing on the edge of the terrace and stretching, the Arsenal football shirt he's wearing riding up to show his belly. He wanders across the grass – not bothered by the wetness because he's wearing shower shoes – and flops down onto the bench near the table Luke and I are sitting at.

He stretches again, yawning, and says, 'I thought I heard something. Thought I'd better come and check it out.'

'It was me,' Luke said. 'I let the door slam. Sorry, mate.'

'Y'all right,' Toby said. 'I'm always saying I'll get up and watch the sunrise.' He tips his head back and closes his eyes. 'Wake me up when it's all beautiful and shit.'

'I think I'm going to go back to bed,' I say.

As soon as I say it I feel overwhelmingly tired. Like I won't even be able to get up the stairs and instead I'll have to curl up on the bench next to Toby.

'Maybe wait a few minutes,' Luke says.

He points up. I look up. The sky is lighter blue, but striped with wispy pink and purple clouds. I take a photo on my phone. At least I've got something to post to Instagram now.

10

'I think Leonie's right,' Mum says later, over breakfast. 'I think we should go. To L'Angelo.'

The Angel. Dad's hotel is called The Angel.

My stomach curls at the thought of walking in there without Dad. Of not hearing his stories – he told some of the same stories every single year. One about walking into a room where a woman was just walking out of the shower, naked. 'I don't know which of us screamed louder.' One about smashing a tray full of glasses on the marble floor and having to stay an extra shift to get it all cleared up. One about a famous actor's wedding where he and the bride stayed in a much fancier hotel, but he put all his family up at L'Angelo.

'I do too,' Elyse says, and I have to pull myself back from my memories. 'I keep thinking about what Leonie said – that we might not all come back again, together. I want to drink to Dad. At his hotel.'

Mum nods, her cheeks pink and her eyes shining. 'It'll be hard,' she says. 'I know. But I think we should do it anyway.'

I don't. I don't think I can. I swallow, trying to make the words come out of my mouth, but then Leonie says, 'You don't have to come if you don't want to, Milly.'

I shake my head. I do. If they're going, I have to go. I know that.

'No, it's okay,' I say, eventually. 'I'll come.'

L'Angelo's entrance is just a door between two shops on a narrow pedestrianised street. But it's an incredibly glamorous door: all white marble and gold trimmings and monogrammed tile on the floor. Once, when Leonie was a toddler, she refused to go inside. She stood with her back pressed to the window of the jeweller's opposite with her eyes wide and her thumb in her mouth, shaking her head. Dad had to carry her in in the end. I feel like doing the same now. I don't want to go inside – and Mum and my sisters are just standing in front of the door, staring. I half hope they've changed their minds too and we can just go back to San Georgio and try again next year. Maybe.

'Come on,' Mum says, eventually, her voice sounding strained.

As soon as we're inside, the hotel's distinctive scent hits me. For years, I'd never smelled it anywhere else, but then someone at work bought Mum an amber candle for Christmas and it immediately made our house smell like L'Angelo. It smells warm and sort of dreamy. I love it.

There's an enormous mirror down one side of the narrow corridor and I drop my head so I'm not tempted to look at my reflection. And then the corridor opens out into the wide foyer with its yellow-and-white striped wallpaper and glass-encased staircase.

'It's so beautiful,' Leonie mumbles. 'I'd forgotten.'

The woman on the reception desk – she's young and I don't recognise her – smiles brightly and asks if she can help, but Mum tells her we're just here for a drink and we head over to the bar on the far left. The bar is part of the foyer, but is darker and low-lit. The yellow striped wallpaper is replaced with dark wood panelling and the floor is carpeted in a deep red. We sink into the brown leather chairs and I let myself breathe, as if the hardest part is over.

Mum reaches for the drinks menu in the middle of the low coffee table and I can see that her hands are shaking. I realise I'm digging my fingers into the leather arms of the chair and so I pull my hands away and tuck them under my thighs.

'What do you girls want to drink?' Mum asks, passing the menu to Elyse, who glances at it and passes it to me.

When we first came, we used to get chocolate milk and it always tasted so much better than chocolate milk at home. But for a few years now, Mum and Dad let us have what Dad always called 'a proper grown-up drink' and we'd each try something different every year.

I stare at the list of drinks: Aperol Spritz, Bloody Mary – which is what Mum always has; she says the L'Angelo Bloody Mary is the best she's ever had – Bellini, Campari, Martini. I kind of want a chocolate milk.

'What are you having?' Elyse asks Mum as I pass the menu to Leonie.

'I'm going to get a negroni,' Mum says. Her voice sounds wrong. Like she had to concentrate to get the words out. Dad always got a negroni.

'Me too,' Elyse says.

'And me,' Leonie says, putting the menu back on the table.

I can't speak, so I just nod.

The waiter comes over – again, a young man I've never seen before – and takes our order and we're still sitting in silence when he brings the drinks: four tumblers of the bright orange liquid over ice, a curl of orange peel decorating each rim, plus little bowls of crisps and pistachios. Dad always hogged the pistachios.

Mum leans forward and picks up her drink and so Elyse, Leonie and I do too. We clink our glasses without speaking. I take a sip, wincing at the bitterness and Leonie says, 'Should we say something? I feel like we should say something.'

'The first time we came here,' Mum says. 'When we weren't sure if we'd work – he was here, I had another year at university and then med school and neither of us really thought long distance . . .' She shakes her head and sips her drink. 'And I hadn't been sure that he was right to come to Rome. I thought maybe he should have stayed at uni. Stayed with me. And then we came here and he was just . . . He was so comfortable. He made everyone laugh. Everyone loved him. He was so happy here. And I knew that he was right. He was really good at doing things that made him happy. I always loved that about him.' Her voice cracks and she looks down at her drink.

'My best memory is the time he came and took me out of school,' Elyse says. 'When I was about thirteen? I'd had breakfast with him that morning and I was really dreading school – you remember when I had that fight with Rachel and she wasn't talking to me? I got to school and I was in DT and

Mr Mahoney came in and said I had to go to the office. And all the way there I was expecting it to be Rachel's mum. But when I got there it was Dad. And we walked out of school and got in the car and we went to the Sheraton near Heathrow. The bar's got a swimming pool and Dad had brought my costume and we swam – you can swim up to the bar, which blew my mind at the time – and then we just hung out all day. Until it was time to go home.'

'I can't believe you never told us that!' Leonie says.

'I didn't even know about that,' Mum says, smiling. 'That's lovely.'

'Mine was after we got Mr Berry,' Leonie says.

Mr Berry was a rabbit we got for Christmas. He was in a box under the tree in the morning and we could see it moving and white fluff poking out through the holes in the sides.

'Not when we first got him – even though that was amazing – but after, I don't know when. It might even have been that first night. I woke up in the night and went downstairs cos I wanted to see if he was okay. Well, I wanted to cuddle him really, but you said I wasn't allowed.'

Mum nods. 'You were quite an aggressive cuddler.'

'I got the step-stool to open the back door. And I was already thinking it had been a bad idea, but I wanted to be brave and do it anyway. And then Dad came out. And I started crying cos I knew I shouldn't have been there and also cos I really, really wanted to see Mr Berry. And Dad opened the door and brought Mr Berry in and we sat in the lounge and we cuddle him together. It was great.' She smiles at us all. 'What about you, Mil?'

'You know about mine,' I say. 'The mixtape.' Dad bought me a Walkman one Christmas, calling it a 'retro classic' and he made me a mixtape of all his favourite songs to go with it.

'Yeah, we already know about that one,' Elyse says. 'You'll have to think of something else. Something we don't know.'

I swirl my drink around, the chunks of ice clinking together, but I can't think of anything. I know there's more – I know there are lots – but my mind feels foggy.

'I can't,' I say. 'I'll think about –'

I'm interrupted by a cry of 'Bella!' and I look up and see Mimo heading towards us. Mimo worked here with Dad, but left a couple of years ago. Mum starts to stand up, but he gently pushes her back into her seat and tuts at her, before picking up her hand and kissing the back of it.

'Look at you!' he says, beaming. 'All so beau-ti-ful! And how you have grown!' He smiles from Elyse to Leonie to me. 'I'm *contentissimo* you are here!'

'Are you working here again, Mimo?' Mum asks, smiling up at him.

He pouts, shaking his head. 'No. Very sadly, no. My job went poof!' He mimes an explosion. 'And you? Do you stay here?' He looks around. 'And where is Dominic?'

I curl forwards in my seat, as if I've been punched.

'Oh,' I hear Mum say. 'Oh.'

I stare down at the red carpet, at my feet in my flip-flops; the pink varnish on my toenails has started to chip. I think about Leonie's black varnish and her plan to write on her nails with chalk.

'Mimo,' I hear Mum say and I can tell she's crying.

'Oh, no,' Mimo says. 'Oh, no, no.'

* * *

In the taxi back to San Georgio, Mum sits in the front, crying quietly. Leonie's face is red and blotchy, Elyse is staring down at her phone, texting frantically, but I can see her hands are shaking.

Mimo had pulled a chair over and sat down with us, holding Mum's hand in both of his while she told him how Dad had gone to sleep one night and just not woken up the next morning. How it was a heart attack, no warning, he probably hadn't known anything about it. Mimo had cried and ordered himself a whiskey and downed it in one and then said over and over how sorry he was. How sorry that Dad had died, how sorry he hadn't known, how sorry he'd upset us all.

He and Mum eventually exchanged numbers and he called us a cab and we left.

Leonie rests her head on my shoulder. 'This is my fault,' she says quietly against my neck.

I shake my head, but I can't speak. My throat feels tight and my heart is actually hurting; I'm holding my hand against my chest. People keep saying it will get easier. But how? How is it ever going to get easier? Dad's heart killed him and broke all of ours.

11

San Georgio is quiet when we get back and Mum goes straight to her room. Toby is lying in the garden with his T-shirt over his face and Leonie flops onto the grass next to him.

'I'm going for a bath,' Elyse tells me, as we both head for the stairs.

I don't reply, just go straight to my and Leonie's room and climb into bed. I don't expect to fall asleep – my throat is still tight and my chest feels hollow and strained – but I must do because I'm woken by the sound of a moped on the street outside and I roll over, stretching down the bed.

When I open my eyes I can tell the light's changed and I guess it's probably early evening. I swing my legs out of bed and stagger to the bathroom. I feel heavy and awkward, the way you do when you get out of the sea or a pool and the water's not holding you up any more. I shower and then, back in the bedroom, open the blinds and the window and look out onto the street.

The bar below is opening up. There are three older men standing outside, smoking, and talking enthusiastically. The air smells like tomatoes and oregano. My stomach rumbles, but I don't want to go downstairs yet. There are clothes all over Leonie's bed, so I start sorting them – hanging some up, putting some in the drawers, throwing her underwear into the laundry basket. I pull the duvet across and pick up Leonie's pillow to fluff it up. Underneath it is a pot of Dad's ashes.

At first I think it's mine and I wonder why she has them, but of course it's her tin, not mine. I leave them where they are and put the pillow back.

I get my own pot out of the bedside table, lift it up in front of my face and whisper, 'Dad. I miss you so much. I wish you were here.'

'Mil?' Leonie says.

I must have fallen asleep again. I groan. I'm still wrapped in a towel with a towel on my head.

'You okay?' Leonie says.

I feel her sit down on the edge of my bed. And then she laughs. 'Did you tidy up?'

'Shut up,' I say.

She lies down next to me.

'Piss off,' I say. 'I'm naked.'

'I'm not though, so it's fine.' She pulls my duvet up over me and then clamps her arm around my waist. 'We're going out,' she says.

'Nope.'

'It wasn't a question. The restaurant's closed. We've all had a shit day. Mum, Alice and Stefano are going to some fancy bar with bespoke cocktails and a tasting menu or something. Toby says he knows a fantastic place we can go to.'

'I'm so not in the mood,' I say, lifting my head high enough to pull the towel away and then dropping back down again.

'Don't worry,' Leonie says. 'I can totally sort that mess out. I'll fix your face too.'

I shove her. 'I just . . . I feel like shit.'

Leonie nuzzles at my shoulder. 'You think I don't? I was the one who said we had to go. But it happened. And you've been wallowing in bed for hours now. So you're going to get up, I'm going to make you look gorgeous, and then we're all going out to get absolutely fucking hammered. Okay?'

'Okay.'

The bar is on a rooftop, lit with string lights hanging between trees (in tubs) around the perimeter, mismatched sofas between them. There's a seating area with metal tables, a dancing area – empty at the moment – plus a huge sandpit with a ping-pong table and a hot tub. The bar itself is in a converted silver jetstream trailer.

'What do you think?' Toby asks me, rearranging some chairs so we can all sit together.

'It's great,' I tell him.

'It's pretty chill,' he says. 'Nice relaxed vibe.'

I look at him, but before I get a chance to comment, Leonie says, 'Pretty chill? Relaxed vibe? Oh, Toby, no.'

Leonie's wearing cut-off jeans with my wedge sandals and her Iron Maiden T-shirt. She's got her sunglasses pushed up on her head and isn't wearing any make-up, apart from bright pink lipstick. She looks fantastic.

'Shut up.' Toby grins at her.

I link my arm through his and cuddle him against me. 'I missed you,' I say, forcefully.

I feel him kiss the top of my head. 'Me too, cuz.'

I shuffle on my seat, pulling at my too-short skirt. I let Leonie talk me into wearing one of her dresses. It's a black swing dress with lace over the top and I'm wearing it with Leonie's ankle boots. She kept insisting it was very Rome, very *La Dolce Vita* and she also did my make-up ('You have to have a smoky eye') and put my hair up, since it was sticking up in all directions anyway. I feel good. But not entirely like myself.

Leonie stands up, waving, and I turn to look where she's looking – Gia is crossing the roof towards us. Elyse is still talking on her phone, walking up and down and gesturing. She doesn't look happy.

Luke heads off to get some beers and Elyse finally gets off the phone and joins us.

'I cannot believe that boy!' Elyse says, sitting down on my other side.

I think at first she's talking about Luke and I wonder what he's done, but then I realise.

'Robbie?'

'Who else did you think I was talking to?' she says. 'He's such a dick.'

'What's he done?'

'Oh, just the flats. He said he was going to talk to this girl from college – see where she wants to live, who with, what we can afford. But he hasn't even called her. And he hasn't even looked at any of the stuff I've sent him. Ugh. I don't want to talk about it.'

94

'Good,' Toby says. 'Cos we're not here to talk. We're here to dance!'

Leonie is the first of us to get up and dance, dragging Toby with her, and then I'm not surprised when Gia goes to join them. Elyse is off somewhere with her phone again. Luke moves round so he's sitting next to me. I can feel warmth coming off him even though we're not touching and it reminds me of that time in Alice's garden. Luke's wearing jeans and a white shirt and he smells like mandarins and basil. I tug at my too-short dress again and shuffle forward so I'm sitting on the edge of the sofa.

'Do you want to dance?' he says, mouth close to my ear.

I shake my head and point down at my boots.

He grins at me and I can tell he doesn't believe that's the reason. I look at his mouth and I want to kiss him. I can tell he knows that too. I picture him kissing that girl in the street – what was she called? Carolina? – to remind myself that Luke isn't interested in me. Luke is just interested in whoever is around at the time. But it doesn't work that way. Instead I feel that pulse in my groin again as I picture his hands underneath her top, his fingers moving. And I'm still staring at his mouth.

'Milly,' I see him say.

I shake my head and start to stand up, wobbling slightly in the unfamiliar boots. Luke touches my arm and I look down at him. He's frowning. I look from the little line between his eyebrows to his mouth. I want to run my thumb along his bottom lip. There's a bit of stubble underneath it and I want to scratch it with my nails.

'Don't run away,' he says.

I blink at him. 'I'm not. I'm just going to the loo.'

'Promise?'

I try to smile, but my face won't cooperate. 'Promise.'

In the bathroom, I stare at myself in the mirror. I don't look like me. But that works because I don't feel like me either. I think about leaving and going home. Not just back to San Georgio, but home to London. Home to my room, to my bed, to my old life. But I can't go back. My old life – the one with Dad in it – doesn't exist any more. And it never will again.

I pat my burning face with cold water and head back out into the bar. Luke isn't where I left him and so I cross the dance floor to where Leonie, Gia and Toby are dancing. It's completely dark now and as we dance I look up at the fairy lights glittering against the sky, like trapped stars. I close my eyes and let the music wash over me. It feels a bit like being on stage – just focussing on the music and not worrying about anything else.

An Italian boy comes up behind me and puts his hands on my hips, pulling me back against him. I drop my head forward and then back to rest on his shoulder and I feel his lips at the base of my neck. I laugh, turning around and pushing him away, gently. He grins at me, his eyes twinkling. He gestures at me to go and dance with him, but I shake my head and dance over to Toby.

'Are you having fun?' Toby yells.

I nod at him, grinning. He looks bright and happy, his hair sticking up in clumps. He's not a great dancer, but he is an enthusiastic one – his shoulders shimmying, elbows flapping out like bird wings, but he grabs me and swings me round and I laugh out loud. I see Leonie dancing with Gia, Elyse on one of the sofas, actually not on her phone for once, talking to an Italian boy, who has his hand on her thigh. I look for Luke, but I can't see him anywhere.

I dance for a while and then flop down on a sofa, wiggling my aching toes in Leonie's boots. A woman appears at the end of the sofa holding a tray covered with shot glasses, each one filled with highlighter-bright yellow liquid. I tug some Euros out of my bag and hold them up to her and she puts four glasses down on the table in front of me. Okay then. I gulp one straight down. It's too thick and sweet and it burns and for a second I'm scared it's going to come straight back up again, but it doesn't. So I down a second one fast before I change my mind.

'What are you doing?' Leonie shouts, appearing in front of me. I don't even know where she came from. 'Come and dance!'

I let her pull me up from the seat and across the dance floor to Gia and Toby. The dance floor is crowded and hot, even though we're outside. People bump into me and Toby grabs my hand and twirls me under his arm. I feel disorientated and dizzy, but I just keep dancing.

I don't know how long I've been dancing when I spot Luke. He's sitting in the same place the two of us were sitting before and he's watching me. He looks sad. I tug myself away from Toby and cross the dance floor.

'Come and dance!' I shout at him.

He shakes his head and says something I can't hear. I stare at his lips, frowning. 'What?'

'I don't dance!' he shouts.

I pull a face at him and reach for his hands, but he pulls them away from me, laughing.

He puts his mouth up to my ear. 'You should drink some water!'

'I'm fine!' I shout. 'Come on!'

He shakes his head again and I think about going back to dance more, but I don't want to go without Luke. I step around the table, banging one of my legs a bit, and drop down onto the seat next to him. He holds a glass of water out to me and I grin at him as I pick up the last shot from the table. My finger slips into the drink and it reminds me of Elyse dipping her finger in Dad's ashes and I want to laugh cos I know Dad would find that hilarious and then I remember that he's dead so he can't and he won't. I down it in one.

Luke is talking to me, but I can't hear.

'What?' I yell.

He puts his mouth to my ear again and I want him to lick it, to suck my earlobe into his mouth and graze it with his teeth.

'Are you okay?' he says.

I turn to look at him. 'I'm fine!'

He smiles, looking down at my mouth. I blink at him. 'You're so gorgeous,' I say.

'What?' he shouts.

I start to say it again, but I decide to show him instead. I slide my fingers into his hair at the side, my thumb grazing the edge of his ear. Maybe I'll suck on his earlobe instead.

'You're so drunk,' he says. Either he's talking right into my ear or someone's turned the music down.

'You should be drunk too,' I tell him. I turn around to give him one of the shots I bought, but they're gone. Someone must've taken them. Bastards.

'Who is?' Luke says.

'What?'

'Who's a bastard?'

'You are,' I mumble, leaning closer until my mouth is just in front of his. If I stuck my tongue out I could lick his bottom lip. 'Such a bastard.'

He pushes me away, his hands in front of my shoulders. He's looking at me really intently and I frown at him.

'What?' The music's definitely quieter now. Neither of us is shouting.

'I don't want to do this when you're drunk,' he says.

'But if I wasn't drunk I wouldn't want to,' I say without thinking. I look down and notice the zip on one of my boots is undone. When did that happen? I pull it up.

He frowns and sort of half-smiles. 'That's flattering.'

I laugh. 'Oh no. Not like that. Of course I'd want to do you! I always want to do you! I mean, I couldn't. If I wasn't drunk. I just wouldn't be able to. It would be too much.'

He gently pushes me back on the sofa, so I'm sitting up and next to him and says, 'You're not too much, Milly. You're never too much.'

I'm still staring at his mouth, but I know he's not going to kiss me and I'm not going to kiss him.

'I have to go,' I say. 'I have to go now.'

'Okay,' he says. 'I can take you.'

I shake my head, but it makes everything look blurry and scary so I stop. 'I can go on my own.'

He laughs. 'That's not happening.'

'Luke,' I say, bending over so my head's almost resting on my knees. 'Why do I keep doing this with you?'

I feel his hand between my shoulders, stroking my back gently. 'I don't know,' he says into my ear. 'But I like you. I've liked you since the first time I met you. And I like you now even though you're drunk and talking shit and you've got ketchup down the front of your dress.'

'Shit!' I say, sitting up and seeing the dried ketchup smeared over the lace part of Leonie's dress. She's going to kill me.

'So I'm going to take you home,' Luke says. 'Stay here a sec, I'm going to find your sisters. And Toby.'

Luke gets up and I drop my head back against the back of the sofa. I could go to sleep. I really want to go to sleep. I close my eyes and my head starts spinning. I hate that.

12

My first thought when I wake up is that I'm going to be sick. But when I try to move, I feel even worse, so I just try to stay very, very still and hope it goes away. My feet hurt. A lot. Actually, everything hurts. I don't remember coming home and I feel that stab of panic that I've probably lost my bag or my phone, but one of my hands is hanging off the bed and I think it's my phone my fingers are resting on.

I try to remember coming home, but there's nothing. The last thing I can remember is eating a hot dog, I think. Something with ketchup, anyway. Ketchup. Something about ketchup tugs at the back of my brain, but I can't quite grab it. I roll over and press my forehead into the pillow. The back of my neck feels crunchy. And my mouth is horribly dry. I feel around the floor next to my phone and find a water bottle. I manage to bring it up into the bed and get the lid off, but when I try to tip my head back to drink some, it feels like my brain is going to burst. I hold onto my forehead with my other hand and force some water down. I've only just got my head back on my pillow when my mouth fills with fluid again and I lurch out of my bed, stagger into the bathroom, and drop to my knees in front of the loo.

Once I've finished throwing up, I haul myself to standing using the sink and let out a squeak of horror when I see my reflection. Obviously I didn't take my make-up off and Leonie's 'smoky eye' is smeared all over the place. I look like a raccoon. A very sick and pasty raccoon. I clean my eyes with a cleansing wipe, but it doesn't really help. The raccoon effect has gone, but I still look sick and pasty.

I stagger back into the bedroom and find Elyse in Leonie's bed, sitting up against the pillows and looking down at her phone. I can see the shape of Leonie under the duvet next to her. Elyse looks up at me and grins.

'Fuck me,' she says. 'You look horrific.'

'Thanks,' I say, wincing.

'Did you just vom?'

I start to nod, but it hurts my neck, my head, my eyeballs. 'Yeah.'

'How many shots did you have?'

'How should I know?'

'I didn't even see you buying them,' she says. And then she snorts and points at me. 'You know who you look like? Voldemort.'

'Don't say his name,' Leonie mumbles, her voice muffled from the duvet being over her head.

'You think You-Know-Who is scary, wait til you see Milly,' Elyse says, but Leonie doesn't even move.

'Why did you sleep in here?' I ask Elyse.

'Didn't want to wake Mum,' she says. And then, 'Luke was worried about you.'

My stomach drops and I clamp my hand over my mouth again, but the sick feeling goes back down.

'Oh god,' I say when I can. I stagger over to my bed and lie down, curling up in a foetal position, shame burning in my stomach.

'What?' Elyse says.

'I don't remember,' I mumble. 'I think I said some stuff.'

'Said stuff?' Leonie says from under the duvet. 'You were trying to lick his face.'

I roll onto my belly and pull my knees up under myself, feeling a stretch in my lower back. 'No, no, no.'

'I mean, he looked pretty into it.'

'I wasn't,' I say.

Was I?

But I remember. Sort of. It feels like it might have been a dream, but I can definitely see his face, close and a bit blurry. And I remember looking at his mouth. His lips. Oh god. Oh god, did I bite his lip?

'I half expected him to be in here when me and Leonie came in, actually,' Elyse says. 'You two got the first cab. He was really keen to get you home. I thought he was on a promise.'

I turn my head away from the pillow. I need to breathe. Or maybe I don't. Maybe I should just lie here until I slowly suffocate.

'Was I dressed?' I say, my stomach flipping with panic. 'When you got back? Did I have clothes on?'

'Fucking hell, Mil, of course you did. You were face down on the bed, drooling and snoring. Your knickers were showing, but you were decent enough. He took your boots off, I think, that's all.'

I have a second of panic that my feet were probably rank, thanks to the boots, but it's soon overwhelmed by the total mortification I feel about Luke bringing me back here, hammered. And whatever the hell I was doing to him at the bar. I think I tried to undo his shirt. I remember laughing because my fingers felt soft and bendy and I couldn't work the buttons. I try to picture his face – was he laughing too? – but all I can see is him frowning at me, looking confused. And then I realise. That wasn't last night. That was last time. After the funeral.

Everyone is slightly hung-over. No one is as bad as me, but none of us is feeling that great. Stefano has made a huge breakfast for us all and we're all slumped around the table, looking rough. Not Luke though. Luke hasn't come down yet.

'You had a good time, then?' Stefano asks us, laughing.

'Great,' Toby says, folding a piece of pastry into his mouth.

'You are an excellent dancer,' Leonie tells him. 'How did I not know that?'

'Dunno,' Toby says. 'I can't believe you've never seen my smooth moves.'

Leonie snorts and tips her head back to down a glass of fresh orange juice.

'What's that?' I ask her, pointing at her neck.

She reaches up and touches the very spot I'm looking at. 'It's a spot, I think,' she says.

Elyse tugs her hand away. 'That's a love bite, Leonieeeee. Mum is going to keeeeel you.'

104

'It's not!' Leonie says, pushing Elyse's hand away. 'It's a spot. And Mum isn't going to see it.' She tugs her top over it, but it falls away immediately. 'And no one's going to tell her. *Capisce?*'

'Shit, all right, don Corleone,' Toby says. 'Who gave it to you, anyway?'

'It's not a love bite,' Leonie says again.

Something flits across my brain. Something to do with last night. With Leonie. But it's gone before I can catch it.

'You're not going to be able to cover that in your dress for the wedding,' Elyse says.

'Shit,' Leonie says, cutting into the frittata that Stefano's just brought out. She turns to Elyse. 'You can cover it with make-up though, right?'

Elyse shrugs. 'I can have a go.'

'Morning!' I hear Toby say and I look up just in time to see Luke coming through the door from upstairs. I feel like my entire body is vibrating with embarrassment and shame. I pick up my latte and hide my face in the enormous cup.

'You rough?' Toby asks him.

Luke sits down next to Toby, so pretty much as far away from me as he can be, yet still at the same table.

'Nah, I'm good,' he says.

I can't bring myself to look at him, focussing instead on the food and coffee. More coffee.

'Have you decided what you're going to do next year?' Elyse asks Toby a bit later, after we've all had coffee and food and are feeling a bit livelier.

'Not yet.' He's still eating toast. He must've had half a loaf by now. 'I think I'll probably take a year out – work here and maybe travel around Europe a bit? Gia's been travelling around as much as she can and it sounds great.'

'Would your mum be okay with that?' I ask him.

He grins. 'She'll have to be. I'm a man now.'

'God,' Elyse says. 'What a terrifying prospect.'

But I'm thinking about what Leonie said. About this possibly being our last summer. If Toby's talking about travelling he won't be here next year. So even if we do come back, it won't be the same. It's never going to be the same.

'What about you, Luke?' Leonie says and kicks me under the table to make sure I'm paying attention. As if there's any chance I wouldn't be.

'I'm going to Liverpool to study English Literature,' Luke says, adding sugar to his coffee.

I feel my mouth drop open.

'No way!' Leonie says. 'Milly's going to Liverpool too!'

'It's not definite,' I say instantly. 'And not to the university.'

'She keeps saying she's not going,' Leonie tells them. 'But she sent back her acceptance just before we left home, so I think she probably is.'

I picture the envelope in the pocket of my suitcase and stare down at my coffee.

'That's so great,' Toby says. 'I remember Dad – I mean your Dom – argh! – I mean your dad . . . sorry. I remember him telling me you were applying, is what I'm trying to say. He was really proud.'

'Yeah, that's cos he went there,' Elyse says.

106

I've got that tight feeling in my throat again. Yes, me and Dad used to talk about it, but I never really expected it to happen. Did I? I can't remember now.

'What do you want to do?' Elyse asks Luke. 'After uni, I mean.'

'Journalism, I think,' he says. 'Or maybe teaching? Not really sure yet. That's one of the things about an English degree – you keep your options open.'

'Yeah, either that or it's completely useless,' Toby says.

Toby asks Elyse about her course and then Luke says, 'Do you know what you want to do, Leonie?'

Leonie's just shoved a huge chunk of frittata in her mouth so she gestures for a couple of seconds and then, crumbs flying, says, 'I'm thinking about medicine.'

'You're what?' I say at the same time as Elyse says, 'Are you?!'

'Yeah, I think so,' Leonie says.

'Since when?' Elyse asks.

'Since . . . you know . . . since Dad,' she says.

Elyse and I stare at her. I had no idea she'd been thinking such a thing and apparently neither did Elyse.

'I just think if there was something I could do to make a difference, you know, to stop the same thing happening to anyone else. Not that I think I'm going to be able to, you know, cure heart disease or whatever, but if I could do some research and make some progress . . .' She picks up a piece of bacon and folds it into her mouth.

'I think that's awesome,' Luke says.

I do too. And it makes me realise again how much Leonie's grown up in the past year without me noticing. It worries me what else I might have missed.

13

'Did you talk to Luke?' Elyse asks me as we walk through the market.

I shake my head. Which is a mistake because I immediately feel sick again. I reach up and press my fingers to my temples.

'You need more water,' Elyse says. 'Did you bring some?'

I squeak out a no and she rolls her eyes and goes to buy one from a market stall. I stand very still, my eyes closed behind my sunglasses. Leonie decided to hang around the restaurant today, but Elyse wants to do some shopping and I didn't want to be anywhere near Luke so I said I'd come with her. I don't like my sisters going out on their own in Rome. Even at home in London I don't like not knowing where they are, but at least I know they are usually with friends. Here it all feels a bit less safe.

I can hear Elyse chatting in Italian with one of the stallholders. Her Italian's always been the best out of all of us – she picks things up really quickly. I open my eyes and squint at her: she's pointing at fruit. I close my eyes again.

'Here,' Elyse says.

I open my eyes as she presses a cold bottle of water into my right hand and an orange into my left. The water bottle is wet with condensation and I press it to my forehead. I feel briefly better.

'Want me to peel that for you?' she asks, already taking the orange off me.

As Elyse peels, I open the water and drink as much as I can. Elyse takes the orange peel back to the stall to throw it away, even though the cobbles are covered with fruit and vegetable peelings and the occasional curl of pasta.

Elyse hooks her arm through mine and turns back towards San Georgio.

'No,' I say, stopping dead. 'I don't want to see Luke.'

'You've already seen him,' Elyse says, rolling her eyes.

'Well, then I don't want to see him again.'

'But I want to go to the fabric shop.'

I steer us back the way we came and say, 'We can walk all the way round.'

We pass the small Cinema Farnese and walk along the edge of the square into a narrow side street.

'Have you had any more luck with a flat?' I ask her, just for something to say. When it's quiet, I focus more on the banging in my head.

'Maybe,' she says. 'I found an amazing one, but it was really expensive and only one bedroom so it would depend.'

'On what?' I say, as she steers me out of the way of an oncoming taxi.

'On whether I use Dad's money.'

'Oh my god,' I say.

'I know,' Elyse says. 'I knew you'd say that, but –'

'No,' I say, looking around desperately, one hand over my mouth. 'I'm going to be sick.'

'Shit,' Elyse says.

I can actually feel the vomit building and I don't know what I'm going to do – or, more importantly, where I'm going to do it – but then I see one of those bins that's just a clear plastic bag hanging from a circle and I dart through the tourists, almost crashing into a man carrying a stack of fruit crates, and yank open the lid and whatever was left from last night reappears.

I feel Elyse rubbing my back and holding back my hair and I hear an English woman say 'Poor you', which makes me feel even worse. All these people here on holiday, out shopping in the sun, subjected to the revolting sounds I'm making.

My eyes are streaming and I cough a bit, but I think I'm done. I stand up, still holding onto the bin, and Elyse hands me a tissue.

'You okay?' she says. 'You're sweating.'

'Ugh,' I groan. I wipe my eyes and mouth and throw the tissue in the bin.

Elyse drops the orange in too. 'Sorry, that wasn't my best idea. I was thinking vitamin C . . . but maybe that's for colds, not hangovers.'

I let go of the bin and hold Elyse's arm instead. I want to get away from the gross mess I've just made and from anyone who may feasibly have seen me making it. We pass a middle-aged couple sitting with espressos at one of the barrel tables and totally judging me.

'God,' Elyse says, as we walk. 'You're shaking.'

'I feel terrible,' I say. 'What is wrong with me?'

'You're hungover, dickhead,' Elyse says.

'I don't mean that,' I say, but I'm interrupted by an Italian man opening the parasols over the tables outside a restaurant. He shouts '*Ciao, bella*!' at Elyse and kisses his fingers.

'*Buongiorno*!' she says and waves at him, even though when men shout at her at home she tells them to fuck off.

'You're different in Italy,' I say, drinking some more water. My mouth tastes disgusting.

'We all are,' Elyse says. 'Hadn't you noticed?'

Actually, yeah, I had. About the rest of us. But not Elyse so much. Not until this trip. Maybe it's because of Dad. Or maybe it's because of Robbie.

'Why do you feel terrible?' Elyse says.

'What?'

'You said you felt terrible, not the hangover. About what?'

There's a few market stalls along the edge of the street and Elyse wanders over and I follow. She picks up a bright yellow leather bag and then turns to look at me. 'Go on.'

'I feel terrible about last night,' I say.

An Italian guy appears from the other side of stall. 'Sixty euro.'

'Thanks,' Elyse says, putting the bag down.

'Very nice bag,' he says and picks it up again, holding it out to her. '*Prego, prego*!'

'No, I don't want it. Thanks,' Elyse says.

He nods and puts the bag back down. Elyse walks to the next stall.

'What about last night?' she asks me.

I follow her around the stall.

'About getting so drunk. And throwing myself at Luke. And having to be brought home. And throwing up, for that matter.'

'Fucksake, Mil,' Elyse says, flicking through a rail of patterned silk dresses. 'You're eighteen. That's all perfectly normal behaviour for an eighteen-year-old, you know.'

'I know,' I say. 'But that doesn't make it right for me.'

'Didn't you ever get hammered at home?' She unhooks a red and brown dress and holds it up against herself, looking down.

I think about what happened after Dad's funeral and my eyes burn, that boulder-in-my-stomach feeling coming straight back.

'Take a photo,' Elyse says, still holding the dress up to herself.

'It's nice,' I say.

'Good. I want to see.'

I take the photo and hand my phone to Elyse so she can see how the dress looks. She frowns and hangs it back up, pulling another one – green and yellow, this time – down from the rail.

'Before Dad, I mean,' she says. 'With Jules and the band? Take another one.'

I take another photo.

'No. I mean, we had a few drinks sometimes, but I never got drunk.'

'I thought Jake was a pothead?'

'Yeah, he is,' I say. 'Well, I mean, I know he smokes. I wouldn't call him a pothead.'

'But you never did?' She takes the first dress down again and holds them up, one in each hand. 'Not even when you were seeing him?'

112

'What?'

'Smoke. Which one do you think?'

'I like them both,' I say. 'And no, I never did. I didn't even know you knew I was seeing him.'

'No?' she says, holding the first dress against herself again. I don't know if she's talking about the dress or Jake. 'Yeah. I saw you with him one day. On the Broadway. You were holding hands.'

She walks round the back of the stall, leaving me standing there on my own.

Me and Jake had been on our way back to our house that day. I'd met him at the station and we were walking home. We said we were going to do homework together, but I think we both knew we weren't. I definitely did. I liked him. He was funny. And nice looking, good looking. I didn't fancy him exactly, but kissing him had been nice. Even if I'd been thinking more about how I was finally – finally! – kissing someone than concentrating on the kiss itself.

In my room, we put our bags down and Jake sat on the chair in front of my desk in the window and sort of swivelled round on it a bit, grinning. He pointed out some stuff in my room, I can't remember what exactly. I know he said I had a lot of books. I sat on the end of my bed and thought about how weird it was. A boy. In my room. Jake, who was my friend. Who I liked. Who made me laugh. In my room. With my bed.

We talked about the band and about Jules. About the gig Jake had been trying to arrange at the summer festival, some fringe thing. But the guy kept ignoring his calls. And I started

113

to think nothing was going to happen, we weren't going to kiss. I didn't know how we'd go from talking like friends to anything else.

And then he said, 'Come here a minute?'

And I walked over to him and he pulled me between his legs and dropped his head back and I kissed him. And he pushed his hand in my hair and I pressed against him until the chair slipped back on its casters and hit my desk and the little bucket I keep my pens in fell off and the pens rolled all over the floor. And we both laughed. And then we were on the bed. I don't remember moving, but we were on the bed.

And I was kissing him and touching him, my hands in his hair, biting at his lip, his ear, his collarbones. And wondering why we hadn't done this sooner. Why hadn't we been doing it for as long as I'd known him? Pulling his T-shirt out of his jeans, stroking the skin on his back, warm and dry and soft. His thigh between my thighs, my hips moving against him.

Rolling on top of him and pushing, pushing, all the time. And it felt amazing. I didn't want to stop. I couldn't stop.

Until he pulled away and kissed me just under my ear and said, 'Calm down, okay?'

And I felt like shit.

I look around the back of the stall and see that Elyse is actually trying on dresses over her clothes, so I open Instagram on my phone and search for Jules's account. Her most recent photos are of her cat, Misha: Misha asleep on the arm of the sofa; Misha on her back with her legs spread; Misha cuddling a tiny toy version of herself. Then there's a selfie: Jules in bed with

Misha's paw on her cheek. The caption says 'I woke up like dis' with the heart-eyes cat emoji. I swipe out of Instagram because I miss her too much. Both of them. Jules and Misha.

'I bought both,' Elyse says, reappearing from behind the stall. 'The fabric shop's just along here.'

We walk for about five minutes and then Elyse says, 'This is it.'

'Are you going to be ages?' I ask her.

'Probably,' she says.

'I'm going to get a coffee then. Is that okay?' There's a coffee shop next door.

'Yeah. I'll come and find you when I'm done.'

She goes inside, stopping in the doorway and looking around as if she's been called to the mothership. I've never really got Elyse's fascination with fabric. One of my earliest memories is of her getting in trouble for stealing some squares of felt from the craft box at primary school. She didn't even make anything with them. She said she just liked the feel of them and once she had them at home, she'd just get them out of their hiding place and touch them.

In the coffee shop, I order my coffee then take my ticket to collect it before taking it over to a small table by the window. I add more sugar than I usually have in the hope that it'll make me feel more awake. Just as I take a sip, my phone buzzes in my pocket and I pull it out to find a message from someone who's not a contact. It says 'Hope you're okay after last night. Luke.'

I stare at it until the letters start to go swimmy in front of my eyes. No 'love'. No kiss. I drink more coffee and think about resting my head down on the table and wishing the entire world away.

I don't know how to reply. Or how he got my number. I text Leonie to ask if she gave it to him and she replies straight away, 'Nah. Prob Tobes. What he say?'

'He hates me,' I reply.

'HE SAID THAT DO YOU WANT ME TO KICK HIS ASS' comes through almost immediately and I laugh, despite the whole wanting-to-die thing.

'No he didn't say it,' I type and forward his text.

I'm halfway down my coffee by the time she replies: 'Not great but this is his first text so maybe playing it cool?'

'Too fucking cool,' I reply. 'I fucked it up.'

'No. He likes you. Come back and talk to him.'

'God no.'

'Want me to talk to him?'

'FUCK NO.'

The next text is six crying-with-laughter emojis. I roll my eyes and click open Facebook to torment myself with Jules's updates, but there's nothing much there either. A link to a petition about saving the bees; a meme about Kim Kardashian; a Throwback Thursday photo of Jules as a toddler – frilly white dress and baby afro in little round bunches tied up with bows. I've seen it before – it's on the mantelpiece at her house.

I used to go to her house after school every Friday. Her mum always made loads of food and her cousins were always dropping in and out, everyone talking and laughing, passing dishes of food around and taking the piss out of Jules cos she's the youngest. I haven't been since Dad died. I couldn't bear it.

I scroll for a while and then go back to Luke's text. I add his contact details and write, 'Bit rough, ngl. Sorry if I was a dick. Ta for getting me home.' I close my eyes and send it before I can change my mind, then I drop the phone in my bag and go and get another coffee, along with a plate of tiny cookies. They're all different and I start with the plainest: round and dusted with sugar. It tastes slightly of almond but mostly of sugar and it melts in my mouth. I eat the rest of the cookies – there's one half dipped in chocolate, another covered with almonds, another sort of like a macaron – and only when they've all gone do I reach into my bag and find my phone.

There's a text from Luke. It says: 'No worries. You were fine. See you later.'

I lean down and rest my head on the table, but I can feel sugar crystals sticking in my skin so I sit back up again and brush them off. I check the time and wonder if Elyse is okay. As soon as I think that, I start imagining that something's happened to her. She's slipped down an escalator or a piece of roof has fallen off and hit her on the head. I imagine an ambulance pulling up outside and me sitting here, not even knowing it's for my sister. If something did happen does she even have any ID? Would they know to come and find me? Or would they just take her off to hospital and I wouldn't even know until I gave up waiting and went to try to find her and –

'What are you doing?' Elyse says as soon as she's through the door. She drops into the seat opposite me, shoving about five bags under the table. 'When I walked past the window you looked like you were having a nightmare with your eyes open.'

I shake my head to chase the visions of Elyse in the back of an ambulance, of Dad being carried out of the house, away. 'Just thinking. You okay? If you want a coffee you have to go up to the counter.'

'Fine,' she says. 'Do you want another?'

I tell her no and while she's gone, I rearrange the bags under the table so they're no longer on my feet and also not so easy to steal. And then I tear open another sugar sachet, pour the sugar on the table and swirl it with my finger.

'Do you want to go back?' Elyse says when she comes back with her coffee and a glass of tap water for me.

'No. Never.'

She laughs. 'Well, that's not really going to work, is it? I don't know why you're in such a state. Everyone gets drunk and does stupid things. It's no big deal.'

'It's a big deal to me,' I say, staring at her.

'The first time Robbie kissed me I had to pull away to throw up,' Elyse says, ripping the top off a sugar sachet.

'You did not,' I say, leaning forward in my seat.

'I did.' She pours the sugar in. 'And then I tried to go right back to kissing him again. But he wasn't keen.'

I laugh. 'I'm not surprised. Weren't you embarrassed?'

'Of course! I really liked him. But he thought it was funny. Gross, but funny. And it was pretty funny. It's fine to be embarrassed. But you're always so ashamed. It's nothing to be ashamed of, you know. We all fuck up. It's called being a person.'

'I'm not ashamed,' I say. 'I'm –' But I am. I am ashamed.

'You are,' Elyse says. 'You've been like this since you were little. You always take things really hard. And that's fine. It's part of who you are. But since Dad it's like you're afraid to make a mistake and so you don't want to live. And then if you do make a mistake – or you just do something, anything – then you can't get over it.'

'That . . .' I frown. 'That's not . . .'

'Yeah, it is,' Elyse says. 'Maybe you need therapy?'

'Oh my god.'

'Oh, come on,' Elyse says. 'I think we should all have therapy. After what happened. Mum certainly should.'

She's right. I think. We probably should have done. But then wouldn't we have to go over and over it? I don't want to go over it. I don't like to think about it at all. Even though I think about it all the time.

14

When we get back to San Georgio, I go straight upstairs for a nap and when I come down a couple of hours later, the restaurant and garden are full of people. It's still a bit early for dinner service and I don't think the restaurant was open for lunch – although knowing Stefano he might have opened if someone asked him nicely enough.

I head back inside to see if I can find someone from my actual family, pushing through the double doors into the kitchen. There's no one around, but I hear a sound that I think is coming from the alcove where the dried food is kept. I take a few steps closer and hear a giggle and then sounds that can only be kissing.

I know it's probably Luke and a girl. Maybe Carolina. Maybe the girl from the moped. Maybe a different girl entirely. So I know I should get out of the kitchen as quickly as possible. But I don't. I keep walking towards the alcove. It's dark – the bright overhead lights are off – and at first I can't work out what I'm seeing. I see Gia's bright blonde hair and I say, 'Toby?' But as soon as the name is out of my mouth, I know it's the wrong one.

'Oh shit,' Leonie says, turning round and pulling her T-shirt down.

'Fucking hell,' I say.

'I was going to tell you,' my sister says, walking towards me, her hands held up in front of her.

I glance at Gia who is still leaning back against the shelves, her lipstick smudged and blurry, her eyes wide and worried.

Leonie grabs my wrists and positions her face directly in front of mine. 'Are you okay?'

'I need . . .' I say, my mouth dry. 'My head . . .'

'Come on,' Leonie says, tugging me out of the alcove and into the kitchen. 'You need a drink.'

'Ugh,' I say. 'No.'

'Pasta,' Leonie says. 'You need a massive, fuck-off bowl of pasta. Let's go and find Toby.'

I take my massive, fuck-off bowl of spaghetti carbonara back up to my room, while Leonie goes to find Elyse.

'What's this about?' Elyse says a bit later, as Leonie pushes her into our room.

'I need to tell you something,' Leonie says. 'Sit down.'

'Do you know what this is about?' Elyse asks me, sitting on the edge of my bed.

I nod, my mouth full of pasta.

'Don't sit there,' Leonie tells Elyse. 'Move up. Sit next to Milly.'

Rolling her eyes and huffing with impatience, Elyse shuffles up the bed and sits next to me, leaning back against the headboard.

'What?' she says.

Leonie sits down on the end of her bed and I see her take a breath and then put her hands on her hips before folding them in her lap and looking over at the two of us.

'I'm gay,' she says.

'Oh!' Elyse says. 'I know.'

'The fuck?' Leonie says at the same time as I say, 'You did?'

Elyse nods. 'Only just. Last night. You and Gia were all over each other.' She shrugs.

'I just walked in on her and Gia in the kitchen,' I say. 'Which is why she's telling us now.'

'I've been wanting to tell you,' Leonie says. 'For so long, honestly. I just . . . I didn't know how.'

'Like that, I'd have said,' Elyse says. 'Just, you know, "I'm gay".'

Leonie nods. 'I know. And I nearly have. So many times. But I just . . . I'm sorry I didn't tell you sooner.'

She tugs at her bottom lip with her finger. 'If I tell you something else, promise you won't freak out.'

'Oh, for fuck's sake,' Elyse says.

'You have to promise!' Leonie says.

'Is it something illegal?' I ask.

Leonie rolls her eyes. 'No.'

'Go on then,' Elyse says.

'Promise!'

'I promise,' I say.

'Me too,' Elyse says. 'But if it does turn out to be something illegal, I'm absolutely going to freak out.'

'It hasn't just been this week,' Leonie says, pushing her chin out, her cheeks flushing pink. 'Me and Gia.'

'What do you mean?' I ask her.

'It started last year,' Leonie says. 'When we were here last summer.'

Elyse and I just stare at her.

'What?' she says.

'I don't get it,' I say. 'So you were together last summer?'

'I mean . . .' Leonie says, tipping her head to one side. 'I don't know if you could say we were together. We kissed and stuff.'

'Last year,' Elyse says.

'Yes,' Leonie says. Her eyes look bright.

'And then again this year?' Elyse says.

'Yes,' Leonie says. 'But also in between.'

I open my mouth and then close it again. 'But –' I manage.

'How?' Elyse says.

'Skype mostly,' Leonie says. 'And Gia came to London a few times. When she could get cheap flights.'

I look at Elyse and she looks as stunned as I feel.

'And I came here once. When you thought I was in Brighton with Gemma and the girls.'

'Oh my god,' I say. 'Why didn't you tell us?'

She looks sad for a second. 'At first I just didn't think it was going to go anywhere. We'd only had a couple of days at the end of the week and even though we said we'd keep in touch, I didn't really think we would. And then after that . . . for a while . . . it was sort of exciting to have a secret. And then I thought I'd left it too late to tell you. I thought you'd be pissed off I hadn't told you sooner. Are you?'

'I mean . . . I sort of wish you had,' I say. 'I wish you'd felt like you could.' My stomach feels hollowed-out again. I can't believe my little sister's had a girlfriend for a year, but didn't tell me.

'No!' Leonie says. 'It's not like that. It's not cos I didn't trust you or anything! I do! I know I can tell you anything. This was just . . . it was nice to have something that was just mine.'

'Oh, fuck off with your youngest-child-syndrome bollocks,' Elyse says, laughing. 'It's not like you got our hand-me-downs – you've always been a right spoilt cow.'

Leonie laughs. 'I know. I didn't mean it like that. I just . . . it was mine. You know?'

And I do know.

When we go back downstairs, the garden is full of people and laughter and music. A bunch of Stefano's relatives turned up to surprise him and then he and Alice phoned some friends to turn it into a bit of a pre-wedding party.

I spot Mum sitting on a bench by herself. She's leaning back and looking up at the sky. The sun on her face makes her look golden and freckled and for a second I want to go and sit on her knee and snuggle my face into her neck like I did when I was little. Instead I sit down next to her.

'Are you okay?'

She turns and smiles at me, but she looks sad. 'He would've loved this so much.'

My throat tightens before I can speak and I have to concentrate on swallowing. Mum has already turned away from me, but I nod anyway. He would have. Family parties were Dad's favourite thing. He loved meeting everyone, talking to them, hearing all their stories, and he loved singing for people too.

'He'd probably be singing by now,' Mum says. '"That's Amore".'

The old Dean Martin song was one of Dad's favourites. He sang it all the time, so there's no way he'd have been able to resist it at an Italian wedding. I nod again.

'I've just had an idea,' Mum says, bumping me with her shoulder.

I know what she's going to say and my stomach clenches in anticipation.

'I know you'd rather not,' she says, 'but I would love it if you'd sing at the wedding.'

I shake my head, but she continues.

'It would mean a lot to Alice and Stefano too, I know it would.'

'I know,' I say and my voice sounds strained. 'I just don't think I can.'

I see Luke coming out into the garden. He's holding a platter of food and looking around. He's wearing long black shorts and a white T-shirt with bright lime-green trainers. He's got sunglasses on top of his head. I want to lick his neck.

'I know you've found it hard to sing since . . .' She stops and takes a breath. 'But I think it might be good for you. I think it might help you move on.'

'Like you've moved on,' I say and I feel, rather than see, her wince.

'I know,' she says. 'You're right. It's funny . . . well, not funny, but . . . actually maybe it is a bit funny. I keep expecting him to come back. I've been letting myself think of him as "away" and I miss him, of course, but I haven't let myself miss him that much because I just kept thinking he's coming back. But he's not.'

I shake my head, digging my fingernails into the wood of the bench.

'I think maybe what happened at L'Angelo was sort of good for me. In a weird way. I need to accept it and get on with my life. Because I don't want to spend the rest of it waiting for him to come back. That would be such a waste. And you not singing . . .' She reaches up and strokes my hair back from my face. 'That's a waste too.'

'I will sing,' I say and it comes out almost like a whisper. 'But I don't think I can do it here.'

There are just too many people. And Luke. Of course, there's Luke.

'That's fair enough,' Mum says. 'I don't think you'll ever have a friendlier audience, though.'

She gestures at the end of the garden and I see Stefano's *nonna*, Vera, dancing with one of the customers who's been coming here since Stefano's father took over from his father. He's as short as Vera and as brown as the bench we're sitting on. They're both beaming at each other.

'I'll think about it,' I say.

'That's all I'm asking,' Mum says. 'He would have been so proud of you.' She reaches out and brushes her fingers through my fringe. 'Going to Liverpool. He always regretted leaving music college.'

'I know,' I say.

I head inside to get a Coke, stopping to say hello to Stefano's various relatives and his and Aunt Alice's friends. Stefano's uncle Paulo takes both of my hands in his, kisses my knuckles and says, 'Look how beautiful you are! Your father would be so proud.' My eyes fill with tears and he immediately hands me his drink. I laugh and he says, 'Do you take alcoholic drink?'

I smile. 'Yeah. But I had too much last night. I don't think I want any today.'

'Ah,' he says. 'That's the best thing!'

I shake my head and go back through the garden, still holding my spaghetti bowl. Vera stops me and hugs me. She's tiny with white hair and big round glasses that make her look a bit like a caterpillar and she's always smiling. Well, almost always. She wasn't smiling when she was saying lovely things about Dad, but only for a minute, then she started remembering stories about him and how much he'd made her laugh.

'Bella Milly,' she says, turning to look over her shoulder, her fingers tight around my wrist. 'You know Carlo?'

I shake my head. 'I don't think so.' It's possible I actually have met him – Stefano has a lot of relatives – but I don't recognise the name.

'You like to know him,' Vera says, reaching up and patting my cheek. '*Molto* handsome.'

The boy that walks up, presumably Carlo, is not actually very handsome. He's a bit funny looking, his features too big for his face, but he's got nice blue eyes and curly dark hair and he's looking down at Vera as if he adores her.

'This is my Carlo,' Vera tells me, patting his cheek like she just patted mine. 'He is . . .' She frowns. 'Not good with girls.'

I glance at Carlo, whose cheeks have gone pink.

'You talk to him, okay?' Vera asks – or rather *tells* – me. She pulls me down to her level, kisses me on both cheeks,

127

enveloping me in a cloud of her powdery perfume, and scurries away.

Carlo's eyes are wide and he looks like he wants to die.

'I'm Milly,' I tell him. 'Have you got a drink?'

'No,' he says. 'I need . . . please.' His accent is strong and I wonder if he speaks much English. If he doesn't, he'd be better off with Elyse, not me.

As we make our way through the crowd, I'm aware of Luke on the other side of the garden. He's talking and laughing and at one point he looks like he's dancing with another older woman I don't know. I watch him touching people as he talks to them. Leaning closer to listen. I want it to be me. I want him to talk to me and touch me like that.

I get drinks for Carlo and me, and Toby gets me to take a tray of pizza bianca back out to the garden. It smells incredible and I snag a piece for myself before everyone descends and grabs the rest.

'We . . . sit?' Carlo says and we walk over to the bench where I sat with mum. She's not there and I can't see her anywhere.

I can't think of anything to say to Carlo, so I eat my pizza bianca and drink my Coke and watch everyone

'You live . . . at London?' Carlo says after a while.

I nod. 'I do, yeah. But I might be moving. To Liverpool.' Saying it out loud makes my stomach twist painfully.

'Ahhh!' he says, beaming. 'The Beatles!'

I laugh. 'Yeah. The Beatles. And football.'

His eyebrows flicker. 'You like the football?'

I shake my head. 'Not really, no. Sorry.'

He nods. His face thoughtful. 'I would say – maybe we go together.'

'To the football?'

'Yes. When . . . commences the new *stagione* . . . season.'

'Oh. Right. Um, no. I won't be in Rome then. We're all just here for the wedding. We go home next week.'

'Yes,' he says, his face still serious. 'Okay.'

I eat some more pizza, but my mouth is dry and I have to gulp some Coke to wash it down. When I glance at Carlo, he's half-turned on the bench and is still looking straight at me.

I have no idea what to say to him. I glance around for my sisters, or even Mum, but I can't see them. And then I see Luke. He's standing on the paved area near the door. He's talking to a woman I don't recognise. She's very glamorous – long dark hair, short skirt, long legs – and I watch as she reaches her hand out and runs her knuckles up his arm before tugging at the end of his hair.

I want to jump up, cross the garden and slap her hand away. I want to grab his arm and tug him inside San Georgio, up the stairs, into my room, onto my bed. I want to –

'Is your boyfriend?' Carlo says.

I tear myself away from staring at Luke and look at Carlo. He's looking over at Luke.

'No,' I say. 'No. Not my boyfriend.'

I'm relieved when Carlo is dragged away by another Stefano relative. He seems nice enough, but I couldn't think of anything to say to him and he seemed to have the same problem with me. So we were just sitting side by side in silence, drinking.

I'm about to get up and find a proper drink when Leonie flops down next to me and hands me a glass of Prosecco.

'Where've you been?' I ask her, resting the cool glass against my hot cheek.

'Oh, here and there,' she says, kicking her shoes off and tucking her feet underneath her. 'Didn't want to interrupt you and lover boy. You looked like you were having a moment.'

I roll my eyes. 'He doesn't really speak much English. He asked if I wanted to go to the football with him – at least, I think that's what he was asking – and that was about it.'

She grins. 'Cute, though. And you know what they say about Italian men.'

'Do I? What?'

She waves a hand. 'Oh, I don't know. But it's probably good. You know, Latin passion and all that.'

'I'll take your word for it,' I say.

'I love this,' she says, gesturing at the party. 'Everyone's been talking to me about Dad.'

'Yeah?'

She nods. 'It's like getting a bit of him back. It's like . . . we have all our stories and we're not going to get any more. I hate that. But these people have their own stories. So, like, that guy –' she points at a tall skinny man with a pointy black beard – 'looks a bit like the devil?' she says.

'Yeah,' I say. 'Who is he?'

'Friend of Stefano's. And he said that he and Stefano and Dad went out one night and got talking to this guy in a bar. He was a tour guide, driving one of those little buggy things? You know, with the open sides?'

I nod. I can't remember what they're called, but I've seen them driving around Rome.

'And Dad convinced him to take them on a tour – this was like 3 a.m. or something? And one of the guy's friends had a buggy with a karaoke machine so they took that instead and they drove and sang round Rome for, like, hours. Till the sun came up. He said it was one of the best nights of his life.'

'That's a really good story,' I say.

And I know what she means. Now I have a new mental picture of Dad. And I can totally see it. I wish I'd been there. I wish I could have been snuggled up against him as he pointed out the sights and sang 'Fly Me to the Moon' or 'You Make Me Feel So Young' or even 'My Way'. And then we would've watched the sunrise and probably got something delicious for breakfast and it would have been my memory. Not the memory of a stranger with a pointy beard I'll never see again.

'And that woman,' Leonie says, pointing at a woman wearing a blue sundress and with a lot of blonde hair piled up on her head. 'She's a musician – she plays guitar, I think she said – and he gave her someone's email address. I can't remember who.'

'That's not such a good story,' I say.

Leonie laughs. 'No, I know. I wasn't really listening. But he was just really nice, you know?'

'But we knew that,' I say. He was just kind. Kind and gentle and properly nice.

'Yeah,' Leonie says. 'But it's nice to know that other people knew that too.'

I nod. 'Yeah,' I agree. 'It is.'

'I need to tell Mum about me and Gia,' Leonie says. 'And, you know. The gay thing.'

'I think telling her about you and Gia will flag that up, to be honest.' I poke at the love bite on Leonie's neck.

'Is it really obvious it's a love bite?' Leonie says, tipping her head back. 'Could I say I did it with hair straighteners?'

'You could,' I say. 'But what's the point if you're telling her about Gia anyway?'

Leonie pulls a face. 'I thought I'd break it to her a bit more gently than "this is where she was sucking on my neck".'

I wrap my arm around my sister's neck and squeeze. 'I'm so proud of you. And Mum'll be fine. However you tell her, she'll be fine.'

Later, I go inside to the bathroom and when I come out, Carlo is walking towards me down the narrow corridor. He smiles when he sees me and I smile back, intending to keep walking out into the garden, but he stops me, his hand on my arm.

'I am . . .' he says, looking at me intently. 'You are very beautiful.'

'Thank you,' I say, but it's barely audible.

'I kiss you now,' he says.

'No,' I say. 'I don't think so, I –'

But he presses his mouth to mine, his hand still holding my arm, his other hand sliding around the back of my neck, his fingers pressing gently.

He's trapped my arm between our bodies and I use it to push him away, dipping my head out of the kiss as soon as I can.

'No,' I say. 'I don't want –'

132

'You don't want kiss?' he says.

I shake my head and look up at him. He looks confused, his blue eyes wide.

'No, I don't. Sorry,' I say.

'You have boyfriend?'

'No.' I push him a little further away and start edging around him, back towards the restaurant. 'No, I don't.'

'So you can kiss?'

I keep edging around him. He's turning his body towards me as I go. 'I can kiss,' I say. 'But I don't want to. Thank you.'

His eyebrows shoot up. 'Ah! I'm sorry. I think . . . I think you want to kiss.'

'No,' I say again. 'Sorry.'

He nods then, his face serious. 'No. I'm sorry. I have . . . misunderstanding.'

'That's okay,' I say, taking a couple of steps backwards so I'm almost in the restaurant. 'Sorry.'

I turn into the restaurant and walk straight into Luke.

'Shit,' I say, as he reaches out to my elbow to steady me. 'Sorry.'

'You okay?' he says.

'Yeah. Thanks. Did you . . . um.' I grab hold of the back of the nearest chair. I need to get some water. It probably wasn't a good idea to drink that Prosecco.

'Did I . . .?'

'Did you, um, see? Anything? Just now?'

He looks confused. 'No? Should I have?'

'No, it's fine. Thanks. Sorry. I'll just . . .' I give him a sort of half wave and then head past him and out into the garden.

But then I stop and turn back. He's still standing where I left him, his hand on the back of the chair I was holding.

'Hey,' I say. 'I'm really sorry about last night.'

Luke holds up his hands up in front of him. 'Not a problem. Seriously. Like I said in the texts.'

'You sounded pissed off in the texts,' I say, before I can change my mind.

His eyebrows shoot up. 'Did I? Shit. Sorry. I didn't mean to. I just didn't want to freak you out. I was trying to be, you know, casual.'

'Ah, I didn't get that. They sounded more "please never contact me again".'

'I should've used an emoji,' Luke says, shaking his head. 'The crying-laughing one? Or the medical mask cos of the vomiting.'

He smiles, the dimple in his cheek popping. I want to poke my little finger into it. I put my hands behind my back.

'How ...' I feel like I'm going to regret asking this, but I ask anyway. 'How do you know about the vomiting?'

'Oh, you didn't vom exactly,' he says. 'In the taxi. You thought you were going to and I think you did a bit, but you ...' He dips his head and scratches the back of his neck as if he's reconsidering telling me.

'What?'

'You said you ... swallowed it.'

'Oh my god,' I say, covering my face with both hands. 'Oh my god!'

Luke grins at me. 'Sorry.'

'Oh my god!' I say again. 'Why did you tell me that?'

134

He shakes his head. 'I don't know. I'm sorry. It didn't happen. I made it up.'

I take a step closer and swat at his arm. He flexes and I roll my eyes.

'Oh, come on,' he says. 'That was one of my best moves.'

'I'm so impressed,' I say. 'I might swoon.'

He grins and I wonder . . . is this flirting? Are we flirting? And then I remember I've watched him flirt with almost everyone here. It doesn't mean anything.

'You've got lipstick on your cheek,' I tell him, smiling.

He grins and wipes his cheek with his thumb. 'I think that was Vera. Have I got pinch marks on the other cheek? Did I get it all?' He turns his face to one side and pushes his tongue into his cheek to give me a clear view. He hasn't and I want to say no and wipe it off myself, but I don't think I can.

'No,' I say.

He doesn't move, but his eyebrows flicker and I force my hand to move up to his face. I watch it move as if it's out of my control. As if it's decided to do something I would never do. My fingers touch his jaw and realise too late that I've lifted the wrong hand – the lipstick mark is on his left cheek and so as I wipe it with my thumb, his lips graze the palm of my hand. I feel a burst of almost-pain, like pins and needles, down my arms and out of my fingers. It's so strong that I genuinely expect to see sparks fly out of my fingertips and I yank my hand back down to grab the back of the chair again. Luke and I are both holding onto it now.

'I'm sorry!' I manage to squeak.

He smiles at me, but he looks confused. I'm not surprised. 'No need to be sorry,' he says. 'Thank you.'

135

I feel my face heating up. 'I didn't give you a shock? I got like a static shock.'

'Oh!' he says. He shakes his head. 'No, I didn't feel it.'

Of course he didn't.

15

When I get up in the morning, the restaurant's empty apart from Elyse, who is sitting in a corner, a coffee in front of her, and her phone face down on the table next to it.

'Robbie?' I say, pointing at it.

She sighs. 'Yeah. He's . . . I don't think we're going to move in together.'

I'm trying to think of an appropriate reaction when she says, 'I know. You can say it.'

'I just think you're better off at home anyway!' I burst out.

'I know you do,' she says. 'You want us all at home. Together. Safe. Life doesn't work like that.'

'I know it doesn't,' I say. 'But maybe it could for a little while?'

'You're not even going to be there,' she says. 'You'll be in Liverpool.'

'Maybe,' I say.

'You keep saying that,' Elyse says. 'But you sent back the acceptance, so –'

'I didn't,' I say, without looking at her. 'I didn't send it back.'

'What? Why?'

'I don't know that I want to go. I need more time. It's in my bag. Upstairs.'

'Oh, fucking hell, Milly!' Elyse says. 'You have to go!'

'Why? Why do I have to? Why can't I just go to UWL? Then I can stay at home and look after Mum and Leonie and –'

'That's why,' Elyse says, shoving her chair back and leaning towards me. 'That's why. You're eighteen. You have to start living your own life. That doesn't mean we won't be a family, it doesn't mean we're not going to be okay. You putting your life on hold is not the answer here.'

'I'm not ready,' I say, my voice low.

'You are,' Elyse says. 'I know you don't think you are, but you are.'

'How do you know?'

'Because you're eighteen. Because you've always been the responsible one. Because you don't want to go, you want to stay home and take care of everyone. But you need to accept that we can look after ourselves.'

I pull her coffee towards me and drink some.

'I'll get you one,' she says, standing and heading over to the kitchen.

Her coffee is too strong and too sweet for me, but I slept so badly that I don't really care. She comes back with fresh coffees for both of us. She turns her phone face up and then back again.

'He hasn't texted?'

She shakes her head. 'No. I gave him an ultimatum. Either we get a place together or it's over.'

'Shit, Elyse!'

'But then I realised I want him to say it's over. I don't want to move in with him. I'm not sure I ever did. I just want . . . something.'

'Something like what?'

'Something for me. Something outside the family. Something to distract me from the fucking great hole in our house.'

I nod, biting at my bottom lip. 'I know.'

At least, I knew that's how I felt. I didn't know that's how Elyse felt. I thought it was weird how different she's been with Robbie, but it didn't cross my mind that this was why.

She reaches across the table and curls her fingers around my wrist.

'We've never talked about it,' I say.

'We didn't think you wanted to.'

'We?' I ask.

'Me and Leonie. We've talked about it. Quite a lot. But you and Mum . . .'

'Yeah,' I say, looking down at the table. 'I don't really want to talk about it now. I mean . . . I will talk about it. When we get home, maybe? But not now.'

'Okay,' she says, carefully.

I pull the fresh cup of coffee towards me and lean forward to smell it, feeling the steam heat my skin.

'So are you going to stay at home?' I ask.

She smiles. 'I haven't decided yet. I might get a place with some friends. It depends.'

'On what?'

'On you and Leonie and Mum.'

I nod. 'Okay.'

We both drink our coffees and then she says, 'So you and Carlo, eh?' and waggles her eyebrows at me.

I close my eyes. 'Oh god. No. There is no me and Carlo. He seems really nice. But . . . no.'

'Still Luke, eh?' she says.

I sigh. 'Yeah.'

'Why don't you just, you know? Grab him. Kiss him. Tell him you want to make sweet, sweet love. Climb him like a tree.'

'God,' I say, laughing. 'Shut up.' And then I feel my throat start to tighten and the next thing I know I'm biting back tears.

'Hey,' Elyse says, tugging at my hand. 'Hey, sorry. I didn't mean to – Of course you don't have to if you don't want to, I just –'

'No,' I say, my voice tiny. 'It's not that. It's . . . I've tried that.' I take a deep breath. 'I've done that. And he said no.'

'Oh,' my sister says. 'Fuck.'

I rub my face. 'God. Okay. I need to tell you. I keep going over and over it in my mind and I just –'

'It's fine,' Elyse says. 'Tell me.'

I nod. And decide the easiest way is just to say it. 'So, after the funeral. When we were back at Alice's?'

I see her nod out of the corner of my eye.

'I went upstairs to the loo and Luke was just coming out of the bathroom. And I'd had a couple of drinks –'

'You drank some brandy, I remember.'

'Ugh, god, yeah. I'd forgotten that. And, I mean, I wasn't drunk, but I wasn't all there either. I felt spaced out. And . . . I just felt sad, you know.'

Elyse reaches over and takes my hand. 'Of course.'

'I mean . . . not just sad. It was more than sad. I remember thinking that I wanted to die too. So I could see him again.'

'Oh, Mil,' my sister says.

I nod. 'So I was upstairs and Luke was there and he said something to me, about Dad. I can't remember what. Something nice. And I kissed him. I just kissed him. And he kissed me back.'

'Leonie said you'd kissed him. That's what she said you were freaking out about.'

'We went into the spare room and we were kissing for a while and then I . . . I wanted more. I wanted to . . . I just wanted to forget about Dad. To stop feeling so sad. And Luke is so –'

'Milly,' Elyse says.

I glance up and see the way she's looking at me – she looks heartbroken – and I look back down at my coffee again.

'I was all over him. I can't remember all of it. But I tried to undo his shirt. And I remember, like, sitting in his lap and trying to push him down on the bed, but he wouldn't. He wouldn't do it.'

'Good for him,' Elyse says.

I nod. 'I know. But then I was just . . . I was so angry. I was angry at everything. And I wanted to have sex with Luke. He was right there and he let me kiss him and I wanted him. But he said no.'

'It's good that he did,' Elyse says. 'A lot of boys wouldn't.'

I drink some coffee. It's not as strong as Elyse's first cup, but it's still got too much sugar in.

'I know. But it was the same with Jake. I . . . we sort of started seeing each other. Ages ago. And then we were in my room and we were kissing on my bed and I . . . I guess I was too into it? And he told me to stop.'

Elyse shakes her head. 'There's no such thing as too into it. Too into it is good. Loads of men would love too into it, never mind a skinny ginger kid like Jake.'

I feel like she's not getting it. She's thinking I was just enthusiastic. But that's not it.

'It's . . . it's like I was totally out of control.'

'But that's okay. That's good. As long as you were enjoying it.'

'I was with Jake.' I stare down at the table. 'And with Luke, even. Even though I shouldn't have been, because of . . . you know. But I was so embarrassed. I'm still so embarrassed. And then when we went to that bar and had those shots and I was just all over him again – Luke, I mean – even though he said no. And . . . I don't even know what's wrong with me.'

'First of all, there's nothing's wrong with you, you stupid cow,' Elyse says, but gently, and the contrast between her words and her tone actually makes me smile. 'It's okay to want to have sex,' she says. 'I mean, it's good that you didn't after the funeral because that would've been weird. But there's nothing wrong with you wanting to have sex with Luke, god!'

Elyse drinks some of her coffee. 'And second of all . . . you can't be in control all the time. That's always been your thing. But it's got so much worse since Dad died. You can't control everything, Milly. And you can't protect everyone.'

'I can try,' I say, staring down into my coffee.

'Yeah, you can,' she says. 'But it's a waste of time. All it does is separate you from everyone.'

'How am I separate?' I say. 'I'm the one trying to keep us all together!'

'But you're trying to keep us together to keep us safe, and life doesn't work like that. We were all together when Dad died!' Her voice cracks and I dig my fingers into my legs.

'We need to be able to live, Mil,' Elyse says, her eyes brimming with tears. 'You know what I keep thinking about? That bit in *Finding* Fucking *Nemo*.'

I smile, knowing that if Dad was here he'd make a joke about that being the full title.

'You know when the dad says something like, "I promised I'd never let anything happen to him" and Dory says that would be awful.'

'And she says it wouldn't be much fun if nothing ever happened to him. I know,' I say. I've watched that film a lot.

'That!' Elyse says, prodding me in the chest. 'Exactly that. You don't want anything to happen to any of us. But it has to. We have to live and we'll make mistakes and we'll get hurt and that has to be okay with you. Because none of us can do it if we're worried about you all the time.'

'You're all worried about me all the time!' I say. 'You have been since Dad died. You all keep saying how I've changed and of course I've changed, but I don't think I've changed that much, I don't think –'

Elyse shakes her head. 'You've changed so much, Mil. You've shut yourself down.'

'I don't think I have,' I say, while a little voice inside is telling me she's absolutely right.

'Remember when you used to watch Dad leave for work?' Elyse says.

I nod. For a while Dad had an evening job, singing in a bar. He'd work during the day, pick me, Leonie and Elyse up from school, make our dinner, and then go back out again, just as Mum came home. And I used to stand on our front step to watch him go. I was always worried he wouldn't come back – I think I'd heard something about bars and thought he was going off to a dangerous job – and if he didn't come back, I wanted to make sure I'd seen him one last time.

'Do you remember when he went without saying goodbye to you and you freaked out?' Elyse asks.

'Yeah,' I say. I try not to. I'd gone to the loo, I think, and when I came downstairs he'd gone. Mum told me he'd tried to wait but he couldn't be late, and I lost it.

'You kept saying, "What if he doesn't come back?"' Elyse says. 'Mum thought you were worried about him leaving us.'

I nod again. 'I remember that night, she came and sat on my bed and asked if any of my friends were upset because their parents had split up.'

'I knew it wasn't that though. I knew you thought he might die. I worried about it too.'

'Did you?'

'Of course,' Elyse says. 'I think everyone worries about that kind of thing sometimes. But you worried about it so much.'

I picture myself standing on our front step. There was a small sort of porch area off to the side and that's where I

144

used to stand, in case someone came out of the door. It had a little wall that I held onto as I watched him go. It was a kind of stone that crumbled a bit when I scraped it with my nails. I did it as I watched him drive away. I wonder if that's where the holding on came from. I wonder if that's where it started.

'But what can I do?' I ask Elyse. 'How can I stop?'

Elyse shakes her head. 'I don't know. I wish I did.'

'You know what I remember thinking? At the funeral? That at least I didn't have to worry about him any more.' My voice cracks halfway through and Elyse pulls me into a hug. The table is digging into my belly.

'That doesn't mean you're glad he's dead,' she says.

'I know,' I say into her hair. 'I miss him so much. But what does that say about me?'

'That you want to keep the people you love safe?' Elyse says. 'That's a good thing. You just need to learn that you can't do it. You can't even keep yourself safe.'

I pull back, sniffing disgustingly, and laugh. 'Good pep talk.'

She grins. 'I was thinking about training as a motivational speaker. But you know what I mean. That Nemo thing. You want things to happen to you. And if things happen to you, some of them will be bad. But that's okay. You'll survive.'

I pull a face at her. 'If you start singing I'll stab you with a spoon.'

'Ooh, who are we stabbing?' Leonie says, appearing through the door from the stairs. Her hair is sticking up at the back and she's wearing her hoodie over Cookie Monster pyjama bottoms.

'I'm stabbing Elyse if she sings "I Will Survive",' I say, picking up my coffee.

'First I was betrayed!' Leonie sings, flinging her arms out to the side.

'It's "afraid",' Elyse says. 'And shut up.'

Leonie shuffles into the kitchen and gets herself a coffee before joining Elyse and me at the table.

'What are we talking about?' she says. Her eyes are still mostly closed.

'About Milly being a big control freak,' Elyse tells her.

'Oh,' Leonie says. 'Yeah.'

I roll my eyes. 'Can we change the subject?'

'Just because you threw yourself at him and he didn't call –'

'He did call,' I say, dropping my head and closing my eyes.

'What?' Elyse says.

'When?' Leonie says.

'After the funeral. After . . . you know.'

'And what did you tell him?' Elyse asks.

'I didn't. I ignored the calls. And he texted. And I told him not to.'

'Fuck me,' Elyse says. 'I can't believe you didn't tell us.'

'I was humiliated!' I say, looking up. 'I felt fucking awful.'

'I know,' Elyse says, reaching over and pinching my arm just above the elbow. 'You know what your problem is?'

'Oh god,' I say. 'Another one? Should I make a list?'

'You think everything has to be for ever,' Elyse says. 'You don't want to go to music college in case you can't make it as a singer. You don't want to even try going out with Luke in case it doesn't work out. And it probably won't work out. And would you even want it to? You're eighteen!'

'You don't get it though, El,' I say. 'It's always been easy for you. You like someone, they like you, you go out with them, you split up, and none of it seems to faze you. I don't know how you do it.'

'It's not always like that,' she says, sliding her phone closer with one finger on the screen. 'With some of them – like Rio – it was just a bit of fun. We liked each other, I fancied him, but I knew there was nothing really in it. With Robbie it was different. I just wanted . . . I just wanted something more secure. I didn't want to go back to college and get off with random boys and never know where I was with any of them. I wanted to not have to think about that. To have a boy to go home to. I told myself he was The One. I don't even believe in The One.'

I don't know if I do either. But I'd like to try to find out.

16

As everyone else gets up, we all congregate in the garden. It's hot already, the air still and heavy, and everyone's tired and slightly hungover, so we're all slumped around, not really talking to each other.

Mum's sitting on the bench reading a Marian Keyes novel. She doesn't really have time to read at home, so she always brings loads of books with her on holiday. Dad used to say she looked forward to the books almost as much as the holiday.

She's wearing a stripy maxi dress and she's got her sunglasses pushed up on her head. She looks better than she has done for a while. More relaxed. Younger. The tension's gone out of her face and shoulders. Even her skin and hair look better. Dad was right: Italy suits her.

I can't concentrate on reading, it's too hot, so I scroll through my phone, switching between Facebook and Instagram and Tumblr. I tap on my contacts and stare at Jules's name, wondering if I can possibly text her after all this time, but instead I scroll back up to 'Dad'.

A few months after he died, Mum sent his mobile off in one of those charity envelopes and I cried all night. I wanted to be able to phone him and leave a message. Or text and pretend he was going to reply. And now, even though the phone's long gone, I can't bring myself to delete his name.

It's like how I sometimes picture him coming round corners or pretend he'll be at home when I get in; as long as his name's in my phone, I could just ring it. Ring it and talk to him. He'd say 'Hey, chicken' and sound really pleased to hear from me. He always sounded pleased to hear from me, no matter what he was doing.

I wish I could talk to him now. I mean, I suppose I could – I know people do talk to their dead relatives, at graves or whatever, and it's not like I haven't had imaginary conversations with him since he died, but I don't know. It seems like we all need to work this out for ourselves. The stuff that's going on now wouldn't be happening – or at least not in the same way – if he hadn't died. So I don't think talking to him about it would work.

I look through Jules's photos again and wonder what it would have been like if I'd stayed in the band. They would've understood if I'd wanted to take some time out, I'm sure. But after Dad I just didn't think I'd ever be able to sing again.

Stefano comes out with Vera and they sit on the terrace, talking animatedly in Italian. Even without understanding what she's saying I can tell Vera is so proud of Stefano – she looks at him with so much love and keeps touching his hands and his face. I feel a pang of envy. We don't see Dad's parents, and Mum's mum died before I was born and her dad has

Parkinson's and Alzheimer's and doesn't really know us any more. For a while, Alice was really keen for him to come out for the wedding, but he's just not up to it.

Carlo comes out and pulls up a chair next to Stefano. He looks over at me and I look away, before feeling guilty and looking back over at him. He's frowning and I smile lightly and do a little half wave. He smiles back and then turns to talk to Vera.

I wonder what it would have been like to kiss him last night. I don't fancy him, but maybe that doesn't matter. Maybe the kiss would've been good anyway. I didn't fancy Jake and then as soon as we kissed it was great. Until it was terrible. But I used to see Jake all the time, so it was mortifying. I could have kissed Carlo and then gone home and probably never had to see him again. Maybe I should have done that.

I glance up at him again, wondering if I should maybe go over and talk to him, but he's talking to Stefano, so I go back to my phone.

Leonie and Gia come out and sit on the grass between me and the bench Mum's sitting on. They sit cross-legged, their knees knocking against each other. Occasionally Leonie bumps Gia with her shoulder and once I notice Gia curling her hand around Leonie's wrist and it makes something flutter in my belly. I want that. But I don't know if I could have it with Luke. Or if Luke would want it with me.

'What time are you heading off?' Stefano asks Gia, eventually.

150

'Soon,' Gia says and I see Leonie's eyebrows pull down. Gia hooks her finger into the hem of Leonie's shorts.

It's the middle of the day. The sun is burning and bright and I have to shield my eyes to see Gia properly.

'You're not staying for the wedding?' Mum asks her.

Gia shakes her head, looking disappointed. 'I can't. It's my parents' twenty-fifth anniversary and they're having a party. And then I have to stay. My sister's having a baby and Mamma's not very well, so they need me to come back.'

'You can come to our anniversaries instead of our wedding,' Stefano says, poking her thigh with his foot.

She smiles at him. 'I will. And I'm so sorry to be leaving you in the middle of the season.'

Stefano scoffs. 'Is no problem. Toby and Luke will have to work hard for once.'

'Twenty-five years,' Alice says, dreamily, ignoring Stefano. 'And they're still happy?'

'Very happy,' Gia says. 'They hold hands still. And Mamma makes Papà's coffee every morning, he makes her hot milk every evening.'

'That's lovely,' Alice says. 'You can make me hot milk every evening, Stefano.'

'Only if you make me coffee in the morning.'

Alice tips her head back and Stefano kisses her neck. 'Nah,' she says. 'You get up too early. You can get your own coffee.'

'Oh no,' Stefano says, nuzzling into her hair. 'The wedding is off.'

'Don't even joke,' Alice says, but without any heat, her eyes closed.

151

'Gia has a VW van,' Stefano tells the rest of us. 'It looks like it will completely fall apart at any time, but she's driven it all over.' He beams at Gia.

'It's fine,' she says, hunching forward over her knees. 'I get it checked out a lot. It's totally safe.'

'Not so comfortable to sleep though,' Stefano says. 'There's a bed in the roof!' He laughs and dips his head against Alice's shoulder. Alice's eyes are closed, but she smiles fondly.

'Mum,' Leonie says. 'I've been wanting to ask you something . . .'

I glance at Elyse to see if she knows what Leonie's talking about, but she's got her head tipped back to the sun, eyes closed, her long hair is fastened up in a messy bun on top of her head and I can see new freckles sprinkling her cheeks and nose.

'Gia says I can work at her family's place for the rest of the summer,' Leonie says. 'And I really want to.'

Mum frowns, putting the book face down on the bench next to her. 'Wait. When?'

'This summer,' Leonie says, shifting up on her knees and leaning towards Mum. 'The rest of the summer. Instead of coming home with you after the wedding, I'd go down to Positano and work at Gia's family's place.'

I look at Gia. She's staring down at the grass, her fingers twisting together.

Mum shakes her head, as if she's still not really understanding. 'Where would you live?'

'Gia has a flat,' Leonie says. 'Gi, tell her.'

Gia looks up at Leonie and then over at Mum. 'My parents would be very happy. We always need extra staff. Especially now. Even if they're probably not good.' She grins.

152

'Hey!' Leonie says, leaning against Gia. She looks up at her and I feel my insides twist, she looks so fond. Then she looks back at Mum. 'I really want to go. I love it here. In Italy, I mean. I don't want to go home yet. Please say yes.'

'I don't think so,' Mum says, frowning.

Leonie's cheeks go pink and I look from her to Mum. Mum gathers her hair back with one hand and then lets it drop down her back, I can see some strands sticking to her neck with sweat.

'Maybe we could all go,' Elyse says, lazily.

She's dropped down onto her back but her eyes are still closed, and she's apparently unaware of the tension simmering between Mum and Leonie. 'I'm not ready to go home yet.'

'That does sound lovely,' Mum says. 'But I have to be back at work.'

'Of course you do,' Leonie says, bitterly. Her hands are balled into fists.

'I'm sorry, Leonie,' Mum says, 'But you know I have to work.'

'You don't need to speak to me like that,' Leonie says, sitting back down, her legs crossed. 'I'm not a child.'

'No, you're not,' Mum says. 'But you're still young, you've just sprung this on me, totally out of the blue . . . and it's not safe.'

'How is it not safe?' Leonie says, shaking her head. 'Gia lives there! Gia's family is there! Of course it's safe. I'm sure it's safer than London.'

'I'm just not comfortable with the idea,' Mum says. She picks up a glass of water from the small metal table next to the bench and drains it.

'But why not?' Leonie says. 'Elyse went away with her friends when she was sixteen.' She reaches out and shoves at Elyse's leg.

'To Newquay,' Mum says.

'So?' Leonie says. 'She was still away. You didn't know what she was getting up to.'

'It's different,' Mum says.

'Because I'm gay?' Leonie says, moving up on her knees again.

'What?' Mum says.

'Leonie . . .' Gia says, quietly.

Elyse sits up and looks over at me. I don't know what to do.

'Is it because I'm gay?' Leonie says, slowly, enunciating every word. 'And Gia is my girlfriend?'

'I- I didn't even know that,' Mum says, looking confused.

'No, I know you didn't,' Leonie says. 'So let me tell you. I'm gay, I've been seeing Gia for a year – since we came out here last summer actually.'

'Leonie,' Gia says again, hooking her hand around Leonie's ankle.

'It's fine,' Leonie tells her. 'She needs to know.'

'Leonie!' Elyse says, sitting up. 'Not like this.'

'It has to be like this,' Leonie tells her. 'Because there's no other way. She doesn't listen. She doesn't hear me.' She turns back to Mum. 'She came to see me at home, you know? No, of course you didn't know. And I flew out here to see her. You didn't know that either, did you? No, because you work all the time and you have no fucking idea what's going on with any of us. So if I want to go to Positano, I don't think you have any right to tell me I can't. Or to tell me anything at all, if I'm honest.'

She stands up, using her hand on Gia's shoulder for leverage, and runs through the garden, past Alice, who's getting up to go to Mum, past Stefano, who's looking at Gia in confusion, past Elyse who's pulled her knees up to her chest, her head bent, and past me.

'Fuck,' I say, quietly, pushing my fingertips into the ground.

'I'm so sorry,' Gia says and follows Leonie inside.

Mum just sits there for a couple of minutes. We're all silent – the only sounds are the church bells nearby. And then she also gets up and goes inside.

'Should we go in?' I ask Elyse, who's lying back down again.

'No. Let them sort it out between them. It's probably time they did anyway. Leonie's been building up to this for a while.'

I shake my head. 'You know what she's like though. I don't want her to go off on one and –'

'This isn't your problem to solve,' Elyse says, her eyes still closed. 'Let them deal with it. They'll be fine.'

I stare at my sister, her face freckled, her long hair piled up on top of her head, the massive sunglasses she got free with a magazine hiding her eyes.

'Fine,' I say.

But the longer I sit there, the more annoyed and restless I feel. I want to go upstairs and find Mum and Leonie and make them sit down and sort it out. But I can't. Because I can't talk about it either. Maybe Elyse is right. Maybe it'll be good for them to get it all out in the open. But I can't just sit here while they do.

'I'm going for a walk,' I tell her.

'Okay,' she says. Her voice is slow and I know she'll probably be asleep before I've even left San Georgio.

I cross Campo de' Fiori towards the Farnese cinema and walk down the side street. It's shady and quieter than the square and I walk slowly, stopping to look in shop windows and down side streets. But I can't stop thinking about Leonie and Mum. I know they'll both be upset – how could they not be – and I feel like I should be with them. But Elyse's right – there's nothing I can do.

The street opens out into a square on the left – the kind Dad loved. There's a small coffee shop/creperie with seats outside and a tiny church. Dad would have gone to look at the church. In fact, he probably did. He could never pass one in Rome. He wasn't great at passing coffee shops either. I think about maybe sitting down and getting a coffee and just imagining Dad's with me, but I realise I've come out without any money. Also that it would be mad.

I keep walking and as the street opens up, I realise where I am. There's a coach party pulled up outside San Carlo ai Catinari, one of my Dad's favourite churches. I think for a second about joining the tour, just following them inside, but I don't want to go in without Dad, so I keep walking towards the tiny garden in the next square.

There's a newsstand, a small florist's, more jewellery and art sellers. And, sitting on the small perimeter wall, Carlo, his elbows on his knees, head hanging down.

'Hey,' I say, as I walk up to him. I worry for a second that it's not actually him, but then he looks up and his face breaks into a smile.

'Ciao.'

I sit down on the wall next to him, but it's too small to be comfortable, so I suggest we move inside the park. We both get up and he follows me around the railings. There's a section of railings that presumably someone's crashed into – there's a big chunk missing and the gap's been filled with orange plastic netting and yellow warning tape. Maybe when we get home we should buy some and wrap it around our house. Or around ourselves.

Inside the park, I sit on a wrought iron bench opposite a stone fountain and Carlo sits next to me.

'I'm sorry,' he says. 'Last night.'

I look at his mouth. 'I'm sorry too.'

'I thought . . .' he says. 'I understand . . . wrong.'

I'm still staring at his mouth. His lips look soft. And I just . . . want. I just want someone to want me. I'm so tired of wanting all the time. I lean forward and press my lips to his. I feel rather than hear his intake of breath and I close my eyes. His lips open a little and I slide my tongue inside his mouth. I don't feel anything. But I want to. So I shift on the seat and press up against him. I feel his hands on my arms and then he's gently pushing me away. No.

I move closer, pressing my chest up against his and opening my mouth wider, my eyes tightly closed. But he's still pulling away. I shake my head. No.

'I think . . .' he says. 'I think you don't want.'

I look down at my hands gripping the metal of the seat either side of my legs, my knuckles white.

'I'm sorry,' I murmur. 'I don't know what's wrong with me.'

'You are sad,' he says, turning the corners of his mouth down.

'Yeah,' I say. 'I am.'

17

When Carlo and I get back to San Georgio, the first person I see is Luke. He's serving customers sitting right at the front on the edge of the square and he looks up and sees me. And then his eyes flicker to Carlo. And back to me.

I want to tell him no, it's not what it looks like. But we're not a couple. And I just kissed Carlo. And by the time we actually reach the restaurant, Luke's gone inside anyway.

I don't know what to say to Carlo, but I don't have to say anything because Mum is sitting just under the awning and calls me over. Carlo waves and goes inside and I sit down opposite Mum.

'Is Leonie with you?' she says.

I shake my head. 'I thought she was with you?'

'She was. But we had a row and she left and . . . I just don't know where she's gone.'

'By herself? Where's Elyse?'

Mum glances over her shoulder into the restaurant. 'In the garden. She says I'm worrying over nothing, that she'll be back soon. I just feel . . . we both said some things.'

I pull my phone out of my pocket. There's nothing from Leonie.

'I've been texting her,' Mum says. 'She hasn't replied.'

Elyse comes outside and sits between me and Mum. 'She'll have gone off to calm down. Like Milly did.'

Mum nods, but her face is tight with worry. 'She was so upset. And angry.'

I'm still holding my phone, so I open WhatsApp to see if she's been online. She hasn't. 'I'll try her,' Elyse says, taking out her own phone and tapping off a message that I hope was at least a little bit sympathetic.

'She'll be back soon,' Elyse tells Mum. 'She never stays angry for long.'

That's true. It's one of the nicest things about her. But I can't help picturing her running out into the road in tears and getting knocked down. Or just being lost. Lost and upset and alone.

'Can I ask you something?' Elyse says.

'Me?' Mum says, picking up her glass of wine and turning it in her fingers. 'Of course.'

'Are you okay with Leonie being gay?'

'God, of course I am!' Mum says, looking genuinely shocked. 'How can you even –'

'I know,' Elyse says. 'I mean, I assumed you would be.'

'It wasn't that. I mean . . . it was a bit of a shock. I hadn't really thought about it, but I don't have a problem with it at all.'

'What, then?' Elyse asks.

Mum drinks some of her wine and then says, 'Your dad . . . he would've been so proud of her.' She smiles, even though she's looking down at the table. 'He would have thrown her a coming-out party! He'd take her to Pride.' She shakes her head.

'You can do all of that,' Elyse says.

'I could,' Mum says, looking up, finally. 'I could. But I just . . . I can't stand that he's not going to get the chance to do it. I can't bear that he's never going to know. I can't bear that I'm finding this out on my own, just me, and I've made such a mess of it. I can't bear any of it.'

My nails are so deeply embedded in my palms that it hurts to uncurl my hands.

'Dominic would have been incredible. And without him . . .' Mum wipes her face with the shredded napkin. 'She flew out here . . . On her own. To see her girlfriend. And she didn't tell me. And I didn't know.'

'So why didn't you just, you know, tell her that?' Elyse says.

Mum shakes her head. 'I know. I should have. I just . . . It was hard. And she assumed that meant that I didn't care. Or wasn't proud of her. But we could've talked about it. We –'

Elyse shakes her head. 'You haven't talked about anything. To any of us. You didn't know I was thinking of moving in with Robbie, did you? Did you know that Leonie wants to be a doctor? Or that Milly hasn't actually sent her acceptance back because she doesn't think she can leave us? Because we're such a fucking mess?'

'Elyse,' Mum says. 'I can't . . .'

'You haven't seen any of us for a year,' Elyse says. 'It's like we lost you too.'

* * *

'Are you worried?' I ask Elyse. Mum's gone inside to talk to Alice, who's been trying to phone Gia, but getting her voicemail.

My sister stretches her arms up over her head. 'Nah. She's probably with Gia. And she's not an idiot. Well, she is an idiot. But I think she can take care of herself. And it's not like this is the first time.'

'That's what I was just thinking,' I say. 'That time me and Dad found her in Starbucks when she was, like, twelve . . .'

'Oh, I was thinking about when she went to the Olympics.'

I blink. 'She did what?'

Elyse looks back at me and wrinkles her nose, before dropping her sunglasses down from where they've been sitting on her head like a headband. 'Shit. I forgot you didn't know about that.'

'What happened? Why didn't you tell me?'

'It was fine. She made me promise not to tell you. She'd arranged to meet some friends in Hyde Park to watch the cycling, I think. Or maybe the swimming? Anyway. She couldn't find her friends and her phone got nicked. She ended up ringing me using some stranger's phone and begging me to come and get her. And it was chaos.'

'I can't believe you didn't tell me!'

Elyse shrugs. 'She thought you'd wang on about it. And you probably would've done, to be fair.'

I roll my eyes. But I know she's right.

'You baby her,' Elyse says. 'You always have.'

'Well,' I say, looking down at the table. 'She's the baby.'

'Not any more.'

No. Not any more.

'She said she wanted an adventure,' I say.

'What?' Elyse says, looking at me across the table.

'Leonie,' I say. 'When we first got here. She said she wanted an adventure.'

'Well,' my sister says. 'I guess this counts.'

Campo de' Fiori is busy with the evening clean-up: the market stalls packing away, the street-sweeper driving around, the tourists and locals wandering out for the *passeggiata*. The air is warm and scented with garlic and roasting tomatoes and a group of children are shrieking with laughter, chasing bouncy balls that light up and flash.

Someone has pulled two tables together right at the edge of the terrace, underneath the awning, and I sit next to Elyse with Aunt Alice and Mum opposite. Mum looks tired, the evening sun shining through the red awning throwing shadows under her eyes.

I look around for Luke and see him on the far side of the terrace, pouring wine and smiling as a customer talks to him. I will him to glance up, to look over at me, and as he puts the wine bottle down he does. I try to make myself smile, but nothing happens. He doesn't smile at me either.

Stefano brings some antipasti out, but I can't eat anything, even though my stomach feels hollow.

'She'll be back before bed,' Elyse says.

'I hope so,' Mum says. She's twisting a napkin between her fingers, torn bits falling onto the table.

I wonder what we'll do if Leonie doesn't come back tonight. Do we call the police? Or is it too soon? Does she have to be missing for twenty-four hours or is it different for tourists? I start picturing the headlines and I have to shake my head to try to get rid of them.

'Is it starting to rain?' Elyse says, peering out over the square. Someone on the opposite side has an umbrella.

'It'll just be a shower,' Alice says, pouring wine for all of us.

The rain gets heavier and heavier. I can see it in the yellow light of the streetlights. The owners of the one market stall that had stayed open run around throwing plastic sheeting over everything, knocking over a stand of touristy mugs in the process. They smash on the cobbles and suddenly I can't catch my breath.

'Are you okay?' Elyse says, peering at me.

I shake my head. I feel like I need to get up and run, but the rain is hammering down and there's a flash of lightning.

'Is it the storm?' Alice says. 'Drink some water.'

I reach for the glass, but my hand's shaking and I knock it over, the chilled water spreading across the table and dripping down onto my legs.

'I'll get a cloth,' Alice says, going inside.

There's a loud crack of thunder and the three of us jump.

'Fucking hell, Leonie,' Elyse mutters. She picks up her phone and starts texting again.

'What are you saying?' Mum asks her.

'I'm telling her to fucking ring me right fucking now.' Elyse puts her phone down on the table and we all stare at it. When, after just a few seconds, it buzzes with a text, Elyse picks it up.

'I am going to kill her,' Elyse says again, staring at the screen.

'Where is she?' Mum says. 'Is she all right?'

'She's fine,' Elyse says. 'She's in Positano.'

18

I hardly slept. Elyse slept in my room and I don't think she slept much either. Whenever I was awake, she seemed to be turning over or turning her pillow over, but we didn't really talk. But we both got up before it was properly light.

Leonie hasn't been in touch and Mum says she was awake for much of the night. We've all left messages for Leonie again this morning, but she hasn't been on WhatsApp since the last time we looked.

'There's a flight,' Stefano tells Mum. 'Takes less than an hour.'

'Yes, but then you have to drive at the other end,' Aunt Alice says. 'You'd need to hire a car.'

'Would it be easier to drive the whole way?' Elyse asks.

Mum shakes her head. 'I'm not happy about you driving that far. I should go.'

Her hair is held back from her face with a headband, there are dark smudges under her bloodshot eyes and she keeps picking up and putting down the same mug of coffee.

She looks at Alice and says, 'I'll be back for the wedding.'

Alice nods. 'I know.'

Mum frowns. 'Oh god, I don't know.' She starts to cry. 'I don't know how I've messed everything up so badly.' She wipes her face with the heels of her hands. 'I know I've been useless. I know how badly I've handled everything . . .'

'Mum,' Elyse says. 'Me and Milly are both old enough to go on our own.'

Mum shakes her head. 'I know you are. I do. I just . . . I couldn't bear it if . . .' She bites her lips and I see Elyse reach for her hand.

'I could go,' Luke says from behind me. I hadn't even realised he was there. I half turn around to look at him, but he's looking from Mum to Aunt Alice. 'If that's okay with Stefano, I mean,' he adds.

'I'm sure that would be okay,' Alice says. 'You don't mind?'

'Of course not,' Luke says. 'If we go now, we can be back this evening.'

I see some of the tension drain out of Mum, her shoulders relaxing, her forehead smoothing out. 'Luke, that would be such a relief, honestly.'

'You can take my car,' Stefano says. 'I have Gia's parents' address.'

'I'm going too,' I say.

'Milly . . .' Mum starts to say.

I shake my head. 'I need to. I can't stay here worrying about her. I need to go too.'

'Is that okay with you?' Mum asks Luke.

And I can't even look at him, because what if he says no?

'It's fine,' I hear him say.

167

'I need to check the car,' Stefano says, standing up and stretching. 'Make sure it will get you there.'

'Stefano!' Aunt Alice says, pouring more coffee into Mum's mug.

'It's fine!' he says, holding his hands up. 'I just mean to make sure it's completely safe. Oil and water and tyres.'

Alice shakes her head, but Stefano wraps his arms around her and pulls her against him, pressing his lips to the top of her head. 'It will be fine,' I hear him say.

'The car is all good,' Stefano says, coming out of the door behind Mum and Alice.

I see Mum look over at me and I can tell she'd been half-hoping the car wouldn't be drivable, that we'd have to find some other way to get to Positano, to Leonie.

'Where's Luke?' she asks Stefano.

'Just gone to pack a bag,' Stefano says. 'And then you should probably go,' he tells me.

I follow him inside and grab my bag and Toby comes out of the kitchen with a box of food and puts it down on the table next to me. I can smell garlic and tomatoes and something else, something sweeter – cinnamon maybe.

Alice hands me a square of card with a phone number and address written on it in Stefano's neat, square handwriting.

'Stefano's cousin,' she says. 'In case you need to stay over. You need to call to get the keys for the flat, but otherwise it should all just be there and ready. It's nice. We've stayed there.'

I look out past the terrace, over the square. The market is setting up: the tiny vans buzzing about with their crates of fruit and veg in the back, the squeak of the metal as they put up the frames, people shouting and laughing. I just want to go.

'Promise me,' Mum says, leaning against Alice. 'You'll call if anything goes wrong?'

'Of course,' I say.

'And as soon as you hear from Leonie?'

'Yes.' I rub the back of my neck. Even though it's early, it's already hot and my hair is heavy.

'And we'll call you if we hear from her,' Alice says. 'And drive really carefully,' she tells Luke.

'I will,' he says. 'I'm a good driver. I promise.'

'And if you hear from her –' she says again.

'Mum,' I say. 'I know. We've been through this. It'll be fine. Don't worry.'

We walk around the corner, Mum clutching at me and Stefano talking to Luke about the car and Toby carrying the box of food and Aunt Alice and Elyse trying to pull Mum away from me.

'You will get back in time for the wedding?' Alice says, as we stop next to the car. It looks fairly new. Not big. Bright blue.

'I'm sure we will,' I say. It's the day after tomorrow. 'I'll make sure we are.'

Aunt Alice nods and pulls me into a hug. 'I just want everyone to be here,' she says into my hair.

'I know,' I say. 'We'll be back. I promise.'

She squeezes me and then pushes me away. 'Now go before I start crying.'

Mum hugs me again. She's crying and Elyse has to pull her away. I feel awful getting into the car, leaving her standing

169

there, but Luke gets in, so I get in and we close the doors, immediately buzzing down the windows because the air inside is hot and still.

'Don't go yet,' I tell Luke.

I look out of the window at my family: Mum, Elyse, Aunt Alice, Toby, Stefano. Dad's gone and now Leonie's gone and now I'm leaving.

'What if something happens?' I say quietly.

'Like what?' Luke says, putting the key in the ignition.

What if we can't find Leonie, I think but don't say.

'What if we die?' I say. 'What if you crash the car and we die?'

Luke frowns and tips his head to one side as he thinks. 'I don't know that there's anything we can do about that. But I'll try really hard not to crash the car and kill us both. How's that?'

'Shit,' I say.

'I know,' he says. 'Sorry, but it's the best I can do.'

'Can we go now?' I say. 'I think we should go. Look at their faces.'

Mum and Aunt Alice are both crying and I wave at them as Luke turns the key and the engine starts. Mum blows a kiss and I blow one back, but Luke's already pulling away and I'm not sure if she sees.

19

'What's that?' Luke says.

We haven't spoken since we set off. My stomach's churning and I'm too hot, even though the car has air conditioning.

'What?' I say.

'In your hand,' he says, nodding at my lap.

'Oh,' I say. I take a deep breath, staring straight ahead. 'That's my dad. Well, my bit of him. Leonie and Elyse and Mum have got a bit too.'

'You brought him,' Luke says, glancing at me and then back at the road.

'Is that weird? It is, isn't it?'

I turn to look at him, but it makes me feel even more wobbly, so I look back at the road. The shutters are down on a few of the shops and they're covered with graffiti. I hated it the first time we came here – I thought it was sad and a bit scary – but now it's just part of Rome.

'Not if it makes you feel better,' he says.

'Has anyone died in your family?' I ask, running my finger along the edge of the pot my dad's in. And then I wonder if that's something normal people want to talk about. But then I guess it's better than not talking at all.

'My mum's mum,' Luke says, glancing over at me and then back to the road. 'She died of cancer before I was born.'

'Your mum must've been young.'

He nods. 'Twenty-eight, I think. And they were very close. Mum says she was her best friend.'

'That's so sad.'

'Yeah. She still misses her a lot, I think. But I've been very lucky otherwise. Still got all my other grandparents. And my dad's grandad's still alive even, but we don't see him.'

'My dad didn't talk to his parents,' I say. 'So we don't see them. I mean, they came to the funeral, but they didn't talk to us. They had a huge row when he dropped out of uni to be with Mum and they never really recovered. We used to see them a bit, but we were never close.'

'That's hard,' Luke says.

I nod. 'Yeah. And . . . it's not like I want to get to know them just because of Dad, but now that he's gone, I wish they were in our lives. They have all these stories. They knew him when he was little. They know everything about him. Up to when he was eighteen. Mum knows pretty much everything after he was eighteen – they met at university – but before that . . .'

'Didn't your dad tell you stuff?'

I glance out of the window and see a building that's being renovated and it's been covered with a picture of how the building looked before. Or maybe how it's going to look after. I like that.

172

'Some stuff, yeah. But now if we have questions, there's no one to ask.' My throat goes tight.

'My mum says that too,' Luke says gently. 'Her dad doesn't remember things the way her mum did. So she says that when her mum died, she lost a part of her history. I mean, she did anyway, I know that. But also the stories.'

I nod. 'Yeah. It sucks.'

'It really does.'

The streets are even wider here, and tree-lined. The buildings are bigger, cleaner, more expensive-looking. We pass a park I remember going to the first time we came. I think we fed some ducks, but I might be misremembering.

'Would you ever contact them?' Luke asks. 'Your grandparents?'

I shake my head. 'I don't think so. I've thought about it. But if Dad had wanted us to know them, he would've contacted them.'

'Maybe,' Luke says. 'Maybe he was just waiting for the right time. I mean, maybe one day he would've done. But now –'

'Yeah,' I say, interrupting. 'I know. And I'm not ruling it out. It's just . . . I don't want to do anything that would've made him unhappy. And I know he wouldn't know.' I twist the pot in my hands. 'But . . . maybe.'

'He was so proud of you, you know?' Luke says. 'You do know that, right?'

I nod. I do know that. And people keep telling me. But it doesn't help as much as people seem to think it will. Because he's still dead.

* * *

'Do you want some music on?' Luke asks, a bit later.

We've reached the outskirts of Rome now and I can see a flyover and enormous blocks of flats in the near distance. I've thought about telling him what happened with Carlo. Telling him nothing happened with Carlo. Because it's him that I want. But I haven't been able to do it.

'Is it okay if we don't?' I say. I like the quiet, the rumbling of the road. And I don't want to be distracted. I want to look out of the window and see Italy. And I want to look at Luke.

The sun is low in the bright blue sky and I watch Luke's hand as he flips down the visor. His fingers are long, his nails short and clean.

We've been driving for about an hour when Luke says, 'I'm just going to stop for a bit, okay?'

I'm glad, because I could really do with a pee. I was wondering when he was going to suggest stopping. We pull off the motorway into the Italian equivalent of motorway services and Luke opens the door and gets out.

I open my door and swing my legs out, stretching them out in front of me before standing and reaching my arms over my head. The sun is low, the air warm. It smells like home – like service stations at home: petrol and grass and hot tarmac.

I turn back to look inside the car for my bag and see Luke's put his hands on his seat and he's leaning over, stretching his back. His shoulders look really strong and I can see his muscles tensing and releasing.

He looks up suddenly – to stretch his neck, I think – but he catches me staring and grins.

'You okay there?'

'Shut up,' I say, trying not to smile. It's the first time I feel like the tight knot in my belly is starting to uncurl.

'I was going to say we should get something to eat, but if you want to climb into the backseat . . .' He waggles his eyebrows at me.

'Shut up,' I say again, but I've failed on the trying-not-to-smile thing.

I open the back door and Luke says 'Wahey!' but I just pull Toby's box towards me and see what he's packed.

'What do you fancy?' I ask Luke.

He opens the back door on his side and reaches for the box, pulling it towards him.

'Hey!' I say. 'I was looking!'

'And now I'm looking,' he says and grins at me.

'Pizza bianca?' he says, peering into a brown paper bag.

'I'll take some of that,' I say.

'And olives and deep-fried aubergine,' he says.

'And that,' I say.

I hold my hand out and he passes me the pizza. I shut the car door and lean back against it, pulling a chunk of the pizza free and folding it into my mouth. I hear the other door shut and then Luke is standing next to me, a tub of olives balanced on his hand. I take one. It tastes like the sea. Luke leans against the car next to me and I can feel the warmth from his arm against mine, even though we're not touching.

'Thank you for this,' I tell him.

'For this?' he says.

I smile. 'No. For driving. For coming with me.'

'I think you've actually come with me,' he says. 'If we're being pedantic.'

'To find my sister though,' I say.

'Yeah,' he says.

We both stare straight ahead and I finally take in the incredibly beautiful view. Fields and hills stretch off into the distance, different shades of green from lime to dark khaki. The sky is still bright blue and dotted with fluffy white clouds. I think about taking a photo for Instagram, but remember yet again that that is not appropriate behaviour when you're on your way to find your missing sister.

'Beautiful, isn't it?' Luke says.

I pull my phone out and take a photo anyway. As if there's no point to taking a picture if you're not going to Instagram it.

'I miss London though,' Luke says.

'I don't,' I say. 'But I love it when I'm there.'

'I think I'm a city person,' he says. 'I like the buzz.'

I nod. 'I like street noise. I like hearing a city waking up.'

'I like looking up at planes,' Luke says.

I barely have to look to know he's smiling – I can see his dimple.

'I like the moon,' I say. 'I never get tired of it.'

'Oh you've gone big,' he says. 'I was going to say I like the escalators on the tube. Especially really early or really late when it's just me. I always pretend it's the end of the world.'

'I like finishing things. Like a tube of toothpaste. Or a bottle of milk. I like throwing it away and getting a new one.'

'I like popping the top on a new jar of coffee.'

'Everyone likes that!' I say.

'Everyone likes the moon!' he retorts.

'Or Nutella.'

'What?'

'Popping the top on a new jar of Nutella.'

'Good call,' he says. 'I like driving. I like driving with the windows down and my music on loud and singing along and no one knowing where I am.'

'I don't like it when no one knows where I am,' I say.

'We're doing things we like, Milly,' he says.

I laugh. 'Okay. I like . . . weeding. I sometimes go out in the garden and pull up the dandelions on the path. Even though they look kind of cheerful. I like how tidy it looks without them.'

'You like order,' Luke says.

'Hmm,' I say.

'You don't like untidiness.'

'Does anyone?'

'Typical middle child.'

'Is it?' I ask, frowning.

'No idea,' Luke says. 'But it seems legit.'

I roll my eyes. 'I think it's all crap, that birth order stuff. People are people with their own personalities.'

'And you don't think those personalities can be shaped by the way you're brought up? Really?'

'Maybe a bit,' I say.

'The bit that makes you love order and hate mess and be scared to start over and want to take care of everyone?'

'Yeah,' I say, eating more pizza. 'That bit.'

'I definitely have the only child thing going on,' Luke says. 'Totally self-centred and self-contained.'

I swallow. 'That's not true at all!'

'It could be!' he says, stepping away and opening the car door. I have to step out of the way too. I watch him pull the box towards him, the muscles moving in his forearm. I spend a lot of time watching his muscles move. You'd think I'd never seen muscles before.

He pulls out a bottle of water and hands it to me before taking another for himself. Muscles in his hand as he unscrews the lid. Muscles in his jaw as he drinks. Muscles in his throat as he swallows. I want him to pour the water over his head and shake himself like a dog. Instead I shake myself. I should probably pour some water over myself too. I'm ridiculous.

We both go inside the service station to use the loos. When I come out, Luke is already waiting for me, leaning back against the wall and scrolling through his phone. I want to walk over and kiss him. Why can't I? He looks up when I'm just a couple of feet away and gives me one of his slow smiles. My belly flutters.

'Any news?' I ask him.

He pushes his phone back in his pocket. 'Just a text from Toby asking how we're getting on.'

'I've just texted Leonie again,' I say. 'But she probably hasn't even got her phone on. She tends to go a bit head-in-the-sand at times like this.'

We walk back outside and I follow Luke to the car. Once we're back on the motorway, Luke suddenly says, 'What's the grossest thing you do that you secretly enjoy?'

I laugh. 'Like what?'

'Cutting your toenails? I love cutting my toenails.'

'Oh my god,' I say. 'That is gross.'

'Cleaning my ears with a cotton bud,' Luke says. 'One of life's greatest pleasures.'

'Ah, we were never allowed to do that,' I say. 'Mum's a doctor, don't forget. Nothing in your ear smaller than your elbow.'

Luke grins. 'I know. I know you're not meant to do it, but it feels so good.'

'Whenever I went to friends' houses when I was little, I always looked in the bathroom and if they had cotton buds, I'd clean my ears. Furtively. And then feel guilty when I got home.'

Luke laughs loudly. 'You rebel, you.'

'I know,' I say, deadpan. 'I was out of control.'

We go opposite ways around a parked car and when we meet again in front of it, I say, 'I like plucking my eyebrows. And sometimes I get a really sharp hair on my lip. I love plucking that one.'

'Oh, now we're talking!' Luke says, glancing over and laughing. 'Tell me another.'

I drop my head to my chest, laughing. 'Flossing. I like flossing.'

'And I'm sure we can both agree there's nothing better than a pee when you've needed one for a while.'

'This is a terrible conversation,' I say. 'Leonie would love it.'

We reach Stefano's car and we're both quiet as we get in and put our seatbelts on. Luke starts the engine and I check my phone again – not only my texts, but Facebook and Twitter and even Instagram. Positano is so beautiful, I'd be amazed if Leonie could resist Instagramming it, but there's nothing.

'I've just thought of a good one,' Luke says, as we pull back out onto the motorway. 'Peeling skin when you've got sunburnt.'

'Oh, gross,' I say. 'Once Elyse burned her nose and it didn't peel but it sort of separated. So there was this crispy bit of skin that we could press like a clicker.'

Luke laughs out loud. 'I once burned my shoulders so badly the skin was coming off in strips. Hurt like hell, but still . . . cool.'

'I like cracking my neck,' I say. 'Particularly . . .' I reach up and press my thumb into the indentation at the base of my skull. 'Just here. I once said "Can you put your thumb in my head hole?" to Elyse and no one let me forget it for . . . well, they've never let me forget it.'

Luke laughs again. 'I like cracking my knuckles. And don't say it'll give me arthritis – my mum says that and I don't think it's even true.'

'I hate that,' I say. 'It gives me the creeps.'

Luke smiles at me and I smile back and keep smiling until he has to look back at the road.

'Where are we?' I say. I must've fallen asleep because the sun is much brighter and my neck is stiff as hell. I stretch it from side to side.

'Want me to stick my thumb in your head hole?' Luke says.

I laugh. 'No, thanks. I'm sorry, I didn't mean to fall asleep. I didn't sleep well last night.'

'That's okay,' he says. 'You know you snore, right?'

'I do not,' I say. Even though I know I do – my sisters have told me.

'You missed a great sea view,' he says, as we head into

another tunnel.

'You should've woken me up,' I say. 'I love a sea view.'

'I'm sorry,' he says, smiling. 'I know how you feel about sunrises, I didn't know it also applied to sea views.'

'Sunsets, sea views, sunrises, the moon,' I say. 'All vitally important.'

'What else?' he says, quietly.

'What?'

'What else is vitally important to you, Milly?'

I want to say 'You. You are important to me,' but I don't even know if it's true. I think it's true. I think I like him, that I want to get to know him better, that I want to spend more time with him, but maybe it's all something I've made up in my head. Maybe I like the idea of him, the fantasy of him, maybe if I let myself be with him, I –

'Have you gone back to sleep?' Luke says.

I laugh. 'Sorry, no. Just thinking. My family. My family is vitally important.'

'I know about that one. What else?'

'No, it's your turn.'

'My mum,' he says.

'Cheating. That's the same as mine.'

'Tough. Your turn.'

'Music,' I say. 'It used to be. But I don't know if it is any more.'

'Music for me too, I'd say,' he says. 'I can't imagine life without it.'

'Oh, well if the criteria is things we can't imagine life without, I'm going to say Starbucks lattes. Twirls. Toast. Netflix.'

'My iPhone. My headphones. My pillow.'

181

'Oh god, yeah. My bed. My brown leather boots. I don't mind when it starts getting cold cos it means I can wear my boots again.'

'Football. Playing, not watching.'

'Cheese on toast.'

'Bacon sandwiches.'

'A can of Coke when you're hungover.'

'A pint of lager on a hot day.'

'A hot chocolate on a cold day.'

'Pizza,' we both say at the same time and then laugh.

We're both quiet for a bit and then Luke says, 'Kissing.'

I bite my bottom lip. I don't know what to say.

'Or,' Luke says, 'more specifically. Kissing you.'

I still can't speak. Or maybe I can and I just don't want to. I want to know what else he might say.

'I know you don't want to talk about it,' he says. 'And we don't have to. But I want you to know that I would like to do it. Again. Kiss you, I mean. Or have you kiss me. Whatever you want.' He glances at me and then back at the road. 'Whatever you want is fine by me. That's all I wanted to say.'

I reach over and press the tip of my finger against the birthmark on his neck and he ducks his head and leans into my hand. I pull it away and immediately wish I hadn't.

'Sorry,' I say.

He looks at me, that line between his eyebrows again. 'I don't know what you want,' he says.

I take a breath. 'I want to kiss you,' I say. 'I want to kiss you all the time. And I'm sorry I've been so weird about it, but it freaks me out how much I like you. And how much I want to kiss you.'

'All the time,' he says, and he's smiling.

'Yeah,' I say.

'That's good to know,' he says.

We're silent for a little while – the only sound is the swish of the tyres on the road – and then Luke says, 'Were you trying to make me jealous with Carlo?'

'Oh god,' I say. 'I'm sorry. There was nothing with Carlo.'

'When I saw you walking back together yesterday . . . God, I thought I'd really fucked up.'

I take a breath. 'I kissed him. First he kissed me and then I kissed him. But . . .' I shake my head. 'It was nothing. It was stupid.'

Luke glances at me then turns back to the road. 'I mostly thought I'd missed my chance. I thought because of what happened at the funeral that you just weren't interested in me any more.'

For a while I can't speak. Luke looks at me again and I shake my head. And then I say, 'I just . . . I'm not good at this. I never have been. And now, since Dad, it's harder. I don't know why, but it is. I know I was a dick to you after . . . and I'm sorry I never called you back. But I was . . . just freaking the fuck out.'

Luke takes one hand from the steering wheel and reaches out to brush his fingers over my wrist. I see a sign for Positano and my stomach flutters again. Part of me thinks Leonie's going to be waiting there for us, crying and contrite, and we can just put her in the car and head back to Rome again. But I can also picture us searching and searching and not finding her, Mum and Aunt Alice getting increasingly distraught.

I suddenly wonder, what if we *don't* find her? What if she doesn't want to be found? What if we never see her again? I curl forward in my seat. I feel like I've been punched.

"You okay?" Luke says.

My phone beeps with a text and I pull it out of my pocket.

"It's Leonie," I tell Luke.

It says. "Let me have one more day. Love you."

20

Once we hit the coast road, neither of us talks for a while. I stare out of the window over the bright blue sparkling water and just try to breathe.

It takes us a while to find the apartment – Positano's roads are narrow and busy and curl back on themselves – and then even longer to find somewhere to park. We would have been fine if we were driving a car half the size of the one we're actually driving, but eventually Luke manages to squeeze it into a parking space and we walk down some steps and then along a narrow cobbled street to Stefano's cousin's building.

He's left the keys for us in a locked box in the foyer and Luke saved the access number on his phone, so it only takes a minute or so until we've got the keys, and we climb two flights of stone stairs to the apartment. Luke opens the door and I follow him in, switching the light on. We're in a big living room with a kitchenette at one end and two huge windows. The curtains are pulled back, but white mesh fabric covers the windows, shading the room from the bright sunlight. I cross the room to see the view and find the balcony.

'This is pretty cool,' Luke says.

I look out over the ocean, at the buildings tumbling down the hillside opposite.

'I think this is the most beautiful place I've ever seen,' I say. It doesn't look real. I feel like I'm looking at a photograph.

'I'm going to get a shower,' Luke says. 'Need to get rid of the smell of the car.'

He doesn't smell – or I haven't been close enough to smell him – but I immediately worry that I smell too and pull open one of the doors leading onto the balcony. A cool breeze immediately washes over me and I shiver. I look at Luke and I find him looking back at me, a small smile tugging at his lips.

'What?'

'Nothing,' he says. 'You look good, that's all. The wind blowing your hair back.' He shakes his own hair back like someone in a shampoo ad and I laugh.

'Go and get your shower.'

Luke picks up his bag and opens the door next to the front door, which turns out to be a cupboard with a Hoover, an ironing board and all sorts of beachy stuff – pool noodles and inflatables.

'This isn't the bathroom,' he says, throwing me a grin over his shoulder.

The next door along is the bedroom and it turns out the bathroom is en suite.

'Just one bedroom,' Luke says.

I cross the room and stand in the doorway. There's a huge window on the left-hand wall and an equally huge double bed underneath it.

Luke opens the wardrobe at the opposite end of the room, next to the door to the bathroom, and pulls out a sort of clear plastic suitcase-shaped bag full of bedding.

'There must be a sofa bed,' he says.

I move out of the doorway as he carries the bag into the lounge and dumps it on the sofa.

'I'll sleep in there,' he says. 'You have the bed.'

I nod. I want to say, 'You can stay in the bedroom with me' but I don't. Because I'm not sure I do want him to stay with me. I picture myself lying in the bed, Luke on the sofa bed on the other side of the wall, and my chest feels tight. I rub the heel of my hand against my sternum.

Luke passes me again on his way to the bathroom and then closes the door behind him.

I shake myself and walk over to the sink in the kitchen area at the end of the lounge, and splash cold water on my face. Luke is just the other side of the wall. In the shower. Naked. Naked and wet in the shower. I could walk into the bathroom and get in the shower with him.

Instead, I step out onto the balcony and sit down on a white metal chair with blue-and-white striped cushions. To the right I'm looking up at the buildings behind us and greenery tumbling down the rocks. Opposite there are more buildings: yellow and peach and white, with balconies covered with plants and window boxes. To the left I can see the sea. Deep blue and sparkling, contrasting with the light blue sky above. I take a deep breath and close my eyes against the sun, then take my phone out and call Mum.

When Luke comes out of the bedroom he's dry and dressed in a white T-shirt and black Adidas shorts with those bright lime-green trainers again. His hair is wet and pushed back off his face and I want to lick him. He sits down opposite me on the balcony, looks over at the view and then smiles at me.

'This isn't so bad.'

I smile back. 'No. It's pretty good.'

'Are we just going to wait for Leonie to get in touch again or . . .'

'Not your style?' Luke says, but he's smiling. He knows it's not.

'I'm not great at confrontation,' I say.

'I'm getting the impression both your sisters have got that covered.'

I nod. And then I realise that he's absolutely right. Leonie and Elyse are both much better at it. I wonder why it skipped me.

'You're the peacemaker,' he says, as if he read my mind. And then I remember Elyse saying the same thing.

'Apparently,' I say.

We sit in silence for a little while, both of us looking out over the view, me constantly checking my phone in case there's another message from Leonie. A sea-gull flies past, squawking wildly and we both laugh.

I look over at Luke and find he's staring back at me, his bottom lip caught between his teeth.

188

'What?' My stomach is already fluttering in anticipation. Plus, he looks really hot.

'When we get to Liverpool,' he says. 'Do you think maybe we could go out?'

I look past him at the sea and take a deep breath. The sea-gull – or, most likely, a different sea-gull – flies past again. I look back at Luke.

'I haven't sent my acceptance back,' I say. 'I told Mum I had, but it's in my bag.'

Luke doesn't say anything and I stay quiet for a while and then say, 'What?'

'But you're going to,' he says.

'I don't know. Elyse says I have to.'

'Well, you don't have to. But you should.'

'I know,' I say. 'I will. When we get home. Maybe.'

I poke my bare toes between the balcony railings, feeling the roughness of the paint on my skin. 'Or . . .'

'Or?' he says, sitting up straighter and leaning his forearms on the table.

Without looking, I can tell he's looking at me. I think he's smiling. I don't look to confirm it because I don't want to lose my nerve.

'Or maybe we could go out here.'

'Here?'

'Yes. Maybe . . . now?'

'Now,' Luke says.

He stands up, pushing his chair back and holding his hand out to me. I think about getting changed. I'm wearing a sundress and flip-flops, but I just want to go, so I don't even look in the mirror as we cross the living room.

I let Luke steer me out of the apartment and then I let go of his hand to follow him down the stairs.

'Wait here,' he says in the foyer.

I lean against the post boxes and watch him go out of the main door into the street.

He walks away, out of sight, and for a second my stomach clenches – is he leaving? But then he's walking back in front of the window again, coming in through the main door and smiling at me.

'Hi,' he says.

'Hi.' I smile back.

'I thought I should come and pick you up properly. You know, like a gentleman.'

I laugh. 'Good thinking.'

'You look beautiful,' he says. And my cheeks heat, my stomach fluttering.

He takes my hand again and this time we head out into the street together.

'Where are we going?' I ask, when he turns right at the end of the road rather than left towards the beach as I expected.

'Little place I know,' he says.

'How?'

He grins at me. 'Google.'

We walk up the hill, my feet skidding slightly on the cobbles, but Luke keeps hold of my hand. At the end of the road there's a small taverna: white with pink bougainvillea tumbling over the front wall, fairy lights twinkling in the large windows. I follow Luke inside, through the restaurant and out onto a small terrace with a trellis like the one at San Georgio and a view down to the bay.

We sit at a table in the corner and I smile at Luke.

'Not bad for a first date,' he says.

'Not bad at all,' I agree. 'You still have to charm me though.'

'Why do I have to charm you? You should charm me – you asked me out!'

'Hmm,' I say. I reach out and take the dark pink rose out of the stem vase in the middle of the table. 'For you,' I say.

He grins at me, takes the flower and tucks it behind his ear. Just then, the waiter comes out and puts two glasses of water on the table before doing a double-take at Luke. But instead of making a snide comment, as I'd expect at home, he kisses the tips of his fingers and says, 'Bella!'

Luke and I both laugh. The waiter leaves drinks menus and goes back inside.

'It actually really suits you,' I tell Luke. And it does – the deep pink of the rose suits his skin and makes his eyes look brighter. 'It's annoying.'

Luke just grins at me then reaches across the table and tangles his fingers with mine.

'This was a good idea,' he says.

'I think I'm going to go,' I say, after the waiter's taken our drinks order.

'Now?' Luke says.

I laugh. And then take a deep breath. 'No, I mean . . . to Liverpool.'

'Yes!' he says, doing an air punch.

I laugh. I like it when he's dorky.

'What changed your mind?'

I look down at my hands. 'Just that . . . I should give it a try. I shouldn't not go just because I'm scared. If I hate it I can just go home. But if I don't go, I'll never know.'

'Sounds sensible,' he says.

'I'm still worried that I'm doing it for my dad, not for me. Because he wanted it for me and I didn't – I don't – want to disappoint him. I don't want to let him down. But I don't want to let myself down either. And that's not a good enough reason not to go. Does that make any sense?'

He nods. 'Of course.'

'I feel like . . .' I turn my glass around in my hands. 'I feel like I've sort of lost myself.' I take a breath. 'You know those buildings in Rome – I saw one when we set off to come here, I'm sure you've seen them – they've got scaffolding up but covered with a picture of what the building looked like before? That's sort of how I feel. Like what happened with Dad sort of . . . demolished me. And I've had this picture up, so I look the same or similar and most people can't tell, but underneath it I'm . . . a wreck.'

Luke is looking at me intently, his pupils dark, but also gently. 'You know,' he says. 'They put those things up when they're repairing or renovating the buildings. So when they take them down, the building's still there underneath, but even better than it was before.'

I shake my head.

'You're still in there, Mil. You're just repairing. And that's okay.'

'But . . .' I say, my voice quivering. 'I don't know how long I need to keep it up.'

'As long as you need to,' Luke says. 'And behind there, you're getting stronger all the time.'

'How do you know?'

'Cos there's, like, thirty men in hard hats working away . . .'

I laugh. 'Oh god. Okay, I think we've taken this analogy as far as it can go.'

'Ah,' Luke says, grinning. 'It's an analogy? Not a fucking metaphor?'

'Definitely not a fucking metaphor.'

I run my thumb along the edge of his hand, pushing my fingers between his fingers.

'So tell me more about these men with hard hats . . .' I say, raising one eyebrow.

He brushes the back of my hand with his thumb. 'I've noticed that you like to have something to hold onto.'

I open my mouth and close it again. No one's noticed that. Not my mum, not my sisters, no one.

'I noticed it when we were in the kitchen the other morning with Toby,' Luke says. 'You were holding onto the table and your knuckles were white. So then I started looking out for it.'

'I do it all the time,' I say, looking down at our hands. His thumb is still gently brushing over my skin.

'Did you do psychology GCSE?' he asks.

I look up at him. 'No.'

'I read this thing – I can't remember exactly what it was – but it was about children with developmental issues learning to walk and being insecure about it. And the therapists had them walk across a room holding onto a thick rope and then they gradually made the rope thinner and thinner until it was just a really fine thread. If they'd fallen the thread would've snapped, but they were holding it and so it was reassuring to them.'

'I totally understand that,' I say.

'And there was this other thing about babies, about how you can hang them on the washing line?'

A laugh bursts out of me. 'I'm pretty sure you're not supposed to do that.'

'I know, right? But apparently their grip is so strong that you could put the washing line in their hands, let go and they'd just dangle there. But if you put their thumbs in their hands they think they're already holding onto something and so if you tried to hang them on the washing line then they'd just . . .'

'Fall on the floor?' I say.

He laughs. 'Yeah.'

'Remind me not to let you look after any babies,' I say and then, inevitably, I blush.

He grins and then turns serious again. 'It's since your dad died, right?'

I nod. I used to do it before. Sometimes, if I was upset. But it's since Dad that I do it all the time.

'I think it's natural, you know?'

'I don't know. I read a bereavement book that said this kind of thing is natural immediately after, but it's been a year and I don't seem to be getting any better.'

'But with your dad it was so sudden. I think that probably makes a difference.' He pushes his hair back from his face and

I feel guilty because for a moment I'm not thinking about my dad, I'm thinking about kissing Luke's neck.

'Maybe,' I say, trying to focus. 'At first, right after he died, it was much worse. I kept getting dizzy spells and thinking the ground was rushing up towards me. That's when I started holding onto stuff. Now I just . . . I think I want to be normal again.'

He shakes his head. 'No such thing.'

'No. I suppose not.'

'But maybe if you try holding on with one hand and maybe holding your thumb with the other hand? See if that helps at all?'

'I just feel like . . .' I know what I want to say, but I don't know if I really should say it. He's going to think I'm completely crazy. Although I suppose he doesn't exactly think I'm sane now. 'I feel like I could float away. Like a balloon.'

He looks at me and I can hear my heartbeat. I've no idea what he's thinking. I wonder if he's going to just get up and go. But then he says, 'I don't think you're going anywhere, Milly.'

After we've eaten, we walk down to the promenade and onto the beach. The sand isn't really sand; it's sort of gravelly and pebbly, and I have to keep shaking my feet to get it out of my flip-flops. We walk towards the water's edge, skirting around a row of bright yellow pedalos.

I take my flip-flops off and let the cool water wash over my feet. Luke bends down and picks something up, then hands it to me.

It's a pebble, smooth and round and warm from the sun. I brush my thumb over it.

'Turn it over,' Luke says.

The other side is pale green with white around the edges. It's smoother and cooler.

'What is this?' I ask Luke.

'A piece of pottery, I think,' he says, bending again before dropping another piece into my hand.

This piece is darker, almost terracotta, and long and thin. The glazed side is pink with black stripes.

'This is amazing,' I say. 'Do you think these are from, like, ancient pottery?'

Luke shakes his head and drops another piece into my hand. It's white with an orange and blue pattern that looks like a fishtail.

'Where are they from?' I say again.

'No idea,' Luke says. 'Pretty cool though, right?'

'I just . . . I want to know where they came from and how old they are.'

Luke shrugs. 'I guess they could be from ancient pottery. Pottery of yore.' He grins at me.

'Stop taking the piss,' I say. 'This is so cool.'

'You know pebbles come from bigger rocks, right?'

'Shut up,' I say.

'Wait till I tell you about sand. I saw it on Tumblr. It's going to blow your mind.'

'Shut up,' I say again. I can't stop smiling.

'Shut me up,' he says.

I feel like something is cracking open inside me. I reach up and brush my thumb along his bottom lip and he stares down at me, his eyes wide. I look at his mouth again.

196

'Milly,' he says, his voice low.

'Do you . . .' I start to say. My voice cracks and I force myself to breathe. 'Do you want to kiss me?'

'God,' he says and laughs. 'I always want to kiss you.'

'Okay,' I say. I slide my hand down to his jaw and then his neck. His skin is warm and soft and I can feel muscles moving under my fingers.

He leans down until his lips are just millimetres away from mine. I can feel his breath.

'Yeah?' he says.

'Please.'

He closes the gap and presses his lips to mine and I feel like I'm filled with light. It's nothing like kissing Carlo. Or Jake. Or even Luke last time. Before, it felt like too much. But this feels exactly right. This feels like what I've been waiting for, what all the wanting was building up to.

His tongue licks across my bottom lip and I shudder, pulling away.

'Sorry,' he says again. 'No pressure.'

'No,' I whisper. 'It's good.' I slide my hand around the back of his neck, my fingers catching under his hair, as I open my mouth and lick a little at his lower lip.

He makes a sound close to a whimper and I pull back, widening my eyes at him.

'So that was embarrassing,' he says, but he's smiling. 'I mean, the flower was one thing, but now you've got me making sounds in a public place, so I'm going to have to ask you to desist.'

'Oh god,' I say, dropping my head and laughing.

I feel his hands on my face, his thumbs sliding behind my ears. He tips my head up to look at him.

'Let's go back to the apartment, yeah?'

I look down at his lips and then I nod. 'Yes, please.'

21

Luke's forehead is resting on the top of my shoulder and I like the weight of it. I want to touch his hair and so, after a second, I do. I reach up and tangle my fingers into it, scratching at his scalp a little.

We're back on the balcony and we've turned our chairs so we're both facing the ocean and can watch the sunset. Beers and crisps are on the table in front of us and neither of us has spoken for a while, but it's not even awkward.

Luke rubs his head on my shoulder like a cat and I laugh. His lips brush against the skin where my neck meets my shoulder and I shiver.

'You cold?' he murmurs.

I shake my head. 'I'm good.'

This is where I would usually stop, I think. Or if I was drunk, where I would straddle him. I'm not sure what to do if I'm not going to do either of those things. I tug at his hair a bit and he groans and it goes straight to my crotch.

'This worked out okay, didn't it?' he says, his voice sleepy and slow.

'What?' I don't know if he means us being in Positano or something else.

'Me and you,' he says. 'Here.'

'It's unexpected,' I say and I feel him smile against my skin.

'I'm falling asleep.' He turns his head and just rests his mouth on my shoulder.

'You could come into my room,' I say. 'For a bit.'

He smiles and says, 'A bit of what?'

I shrug my shoulder, shifting him off. 'Shut up. I mean for a while.'

'Okay,' he says, his voice low.

The bedroom is dark, but there's a strip of light shining on the bed from the street lamp directly outside. I want Luke to lie down in it. I want to lie down with him.

He stands just inside the door, looking at me.

'Don't be weird,' I tell him. 'Sit down.'

'On the bed?'

I nod and he sits at the top of the bed, his back to the headboard. I walk around to the other side and sit next to him.

'I don't know what's going to happen. When we get home,' I tell him.

'Okay,' he says.

I glance at him and find he's looking right at me. I look down at my feet on the bed.

'I like you,' I say. 'But . . . I think I need to work some things out before we . . . you know.'

'Yeah,' he says. 'If you can't say it, I don't think you should do it.'

I glance at him again and he's smiling, his dimple like an apostrophe.

I laugh. 'I know. I'm pathetic.'

'You're not,' he says and reaches down to stroke the back of my hand with his thumb. 'I want you to be sure. Why wouldn't I?'

I nod. 'You're right. It's just . . . you know that I do want to, right?'

He laughs. 'You've made that pretty clear once or twice, yeah.'

'Ugh,' I say, tipping my head back so it bangs on the headboard.

'Not ugh,' he says, reaching over and brushing his hand through my hair. 'Really, really good.'

Our faces are close now, only a couple of inches between us, so close that I can see an extra eye on the bridge of his nose. I smile and touch it with my finger, making it disappear.

'What?' he says and I feel his breath on my face. It smells like beer and lemon.

'You had an extra eye.'

'Ah,' he says. 'That happens sometimes. So embarrassing.'

I laugh and then, without even consciously deciding to do it, I'm kissing him again. He makes a little huff sound against my mouth, but he doesn't stop me and one of his hands moves up to rest on my waist. It feels hot, even through my dress. I shift on the bed, turning my torso towards him and slide my left hand into his hair.

I lick over his bottom lip again and then suck it onto my mouth a little. He groans and it sends a thrill through my body so intense that I think I'm going to have to stop. It's better than it was with Jake. With Jake I was turned on by what we were doing, but not by him. With Luke . . . I want to investigate every bit of his skin.

I breathe against his mouth and open my eyes for a second. His eyes are closed, long eyelashes fanning out over his cheeks and I want to kiss his eyelids, his cheeks, his jaw, his neck. I press a hand to his chest and use it as leverage to push myself back out of the kiss.

'Okay?' he says, eyes fluttering open.

'Yeah,' I say. 'I think . . . Can we maybe lie down and just –'

'Cuddle?'

'Yeah.'

He starts scooting down the bed and I scoot down next to him, holding my dress down so it doesn't ruck up. I feel the heat of him all down one side and I just lie there for a second and let myself get used to it. He doesn't move at all.

'Can I ask you something?' I say.

'Course.'

'The first night we got to Rome, we saw you with a girl.'

'Ah,' he says, shifting slightly on the bed, making the springs creak.

'You were kissing her. Up against a wall.'

As soon as I picture it – his hand under her top, fingers moving over her nipple – I feel that pulse between my legs. I cross my ankles and squeeze my thighs together.

'Carolina,' he says. Caro-LEE-na.

'Yeah. Toby told me. So you and she aren't . . .'

'No,' he says. 'We were for a bit. But it wasn't serious. I mean, it couldn't be, I was only going to be in Rome for the summer.

'And then we saw you again with another girl. Getting on a moped?'

'Oh yeah. That was . . .' There's a silence.

'Oh my god,' I say, twisting to look at him. 'You've forgotten her name!'

'I haven't forgotten it. It's just gone out of my head right now. You're putting me under pressure.'

'Yeah, you're right,' I say. 'I shouldn't expect you to remember the last two girls you hooked up with, that's so unfair of me.'

'You're being sarcastic now, right?' he says and I can hear the smile in his voice.

I laugh. 'Fuck off.'

'Maria!' he says. 'That was Maria. Maria with the moped.'

'That's a handy reminder.'

'I didn't need a reminder. Maria. Similar situation to Carolina, really. Did you have a question?'

'Just . . .' I bite my lip, finding a loose tag of skin and worrying it with my teeth. 'You knew I was in Rome. Did you want me to see?'

Luke blows out a breath. 'Fuck.'

I roll onto my side and look at him in the half-light. He's still on his back, looking up at the ceiling.

'I didn't, like, plan it,' he says. 'But I'd be lying if I said I didn't think about you seeing me with them. Both of them.'

'Because you wanted to hurt me?' I ask. My voice comes out small and squeaky and I want to kick myself.

'I think . . . no. Not really that I wanted to hurt you. I – I mean, I didn't sit down and think about this. Like, I didn't

203

go out with Carolina thinking that maybe you'd see us. But I think it was in the back of my mind that if you did see us it might, like . . . focus your mind.'

I roll back onto my back and join Luke in looking up at the ceiling.

'I know that sounds shitty,' Luke says. 'But, yeah, I was kind of . . . trying to make you jealous.'

There's a thin crack in the ceiling and I follow it with my eyes, wondering what would happen if it gave in. If the ceiling fell in and buried me and Luke in the rubble and we'd be found on the bed together.

'Can we talk about what happened after the funeral?' he says, gently.

I feel a flicker of shame in my stomach and I want to tell him no.

'Yes,' I say, my face heating.

'It was good,' he says. 'I think . . . I think you thought I stopped you because I wasn't into it.'

I close my eyes. I think I can talk about it, but I absolutely can't look at him while I talk about it.

'That wasn't why,' he says. 'I wanted you too. I called you. After the funeral. I called more than once.'

'I know,' I say, quietly. 'I'm sorry.'

'I broke up with Hannah.'

'I know,' I say. 'Toby told me.'

'No, I mean, I broke up with Hannah because of what happened. Because I wanted to be with you.'

'Oh my god,' I say. I feel like something is cracking inside me. How did I fuck everything up so badly?

'I like you, Milly,' Luke says. 'But I don't want to be a distraction. I don't want to be someone you have to get drunk to be with. If anything's going to happen between us, I want you to know exactly what you're doing and be happy about it.'

'I don't –' I start. 'It's just hard for me. All of this. Particularly now. I don't . . . I don't want to get hurt.'

'I know,' Luke says. 'Me neither.'

22

I'm already scared when I wake up. My heart is racing and I can feel myself trembling, but I don't know why. I try to remember if I had a nightmare, but I can't remember anything, there's just this overwhelming feeling of fear. I roll onto my side and pull my legs up to my chest, wrapping my arms around them. And then I hear a sound of smashing – they're collecting the recycling outside, I think – and I know that's what it was that woke me.

I try to get back to sleep, but I feel wide awake. And I'm scared of dreaming about Dad, about that day. I scroll through my phone for a while and eventually find myself scrolling back to photos when Dad was still alive. Last year in Rome. I haven't looked at them since he died. I haven't looked at any photos of him, if I can help it. There are pictures up around the house and I glance at them sometimes, but I haven't been able to really look.

I tap a Rome photo that I can see from the thumbnail is of Dad and as soon as it opens, my breath catches. I close my eyes and try to breathe, then I open them and look. It was taken in the garden at San Georgio, the trellis is showing behind Dad and there's a bright orange Aperol Spritz on the table in front of him. He's wearing one of his favourite shirts – an almost Hawaiian-looking thing, pale blue with big white flowers. He's smiling directly into the camera and his forehead and cheekbones are sunburnt.

He looks so alive, so happy, so Dad. Before I can change my mind, I upload it to Instagram and type 'I miss you' and add a broken heart emoji.

I stare at Jules's contact page in my phone. I could tap on FaceTime and be talking to her – to her face – in seconds. But we haven't done that for so long. Not since before Dad died, I don't think. I remember her calling a few times after, but I just ignored her. And then I turned my phone off for a while. Weeks.

I could send her an email, but we never really did that – unless it was e-invites or something but even that was more often a Facebook thing – so it would be weird. I could message on Facebook, but that seems too distant too. I open WhatsApp and scroll down to access archived chats.

And there's Jules. In her little circle. She's changed her photo since I've last messaged her on here. But when I see the date I'm not surprised – it's eight months ago. Her new photo's cute: she's wearing red lipstick and sunglasses and she's got a huge red flower tucked into her short Afro.

Her last message to me just says 'Hope you're okay' and my chest tightens because I didn't even reply. I know if I scroll back I'll see a few other messages I didn't reply to either and I can't bear it. She kept trying and I just ignored it. And her.

207

It was the same at school. At first she would go out of her way to ask if I wanted to talk about it. Then she'd ask if I wanted to be distracted. And then she said to tell her what I wanted. And then, eventually, she stopped asking. I'd eat lunch on my own, usually in an empty classroom, and we stopped hanging out altogether.

But I miss her. And I miss the band. And most of all I miss the me I used to be.

So I tap the message box. And I type. 'I'm sorry. I miss you.'

And I hit send before I can change my mind.

I get out of bed, pull on yesterday's sundress, and tiptoe through the lounge. Luke is fast asleep on the sofa bed; the duvet and, as far as I can tell, a pillow pulled up almost over his head. I pause for a second and make sure I can see that he's breathing – the cover is moving up and down slowly – then I tiptoe out onto the balcony. We left the door propped open last night because the apartment was so warm, and I'm glad – I don't need to worry about opening the door and waking Luke.

The sky is brightening blue with some pink and peach between the clouds. The early sun is spreading over the buildings opposite like honey. It's cool and I wish I'd thought to bring a hoodie or a blanket out with me, but instead I wrap my arms around myself and just stare out at the sea.

I've never been able to remember what woke me that morning. I've tried, but it's as if I was fast asleep and then instantly wide awake and everything had changed. Everything. I think about it a lot. How if Dad hadn't died, I would've carried on sleeping – oh, I might've woken up to turn my pillow or cos my T-shirt had got rucked up, but I could easily have just stayed asleep. And then I'd have woken in the morning when my alarm went off. I would probably have snoozed it. But eventually I would've dragged myself out of bed and into the shower and then, on the way downstairs, I would've smelled coffee brewing and heard Dad singing. 'Ain't No Sunshine', maybe. Or something by Tom Jones – he used to sing Tom Jones quite often in the morning, said it got his pipes going.

I wish I could remember the weather. If I could remember the weather, it'd be easier to think of what he'd have been singing. Maybe 'Weather With You' by Crowded House. It could easily have been that one. But I don't remember the weather.

I remember Mum shouting. I think that was the first thing I heard. Or maybe it was a door slamming. No, not slamming, banging back against the wall. To Mum and Dad's room, I think. But I was already awake. So it must've been the lorry coming to empty the recycling from the pub a couple of doors down. It happened every week back then until too many people complained and they stopped. It didn't always wake me, but it must've done that day.

Elyse was the first of us to go in there. And then I heard Mum shouting at her to get out. And then there was sobbing. I remember the sobbing, but I don't know if it was Mum or Elyse.

I knew Dad was dead, I remember that. I don't even remember thinking it, I just remember knowing. The sound Mum was making – I could hear Elyse by then, saying, 'Mum, Mum', over and over. And then Leonie was in my doorway, her eyes wide, her hair all over the place. She was wearing a Spongebob T-shirt over red knickers and she looked terrified.

Absolutely terrified. And I told myself that I was the older sister. I should take care of her, tell her it was going to be okay, but I just sat there, staring back at her, my fingers grabbing the duvet and after a couple of seconds she left again, went to Mum and Dad's room.

I remember hearing Elyse ask Leonie if I was still asleep, but I didn't hear what Leonie said. And then Elyse was at my door and she was sobbing so hard she couldn't properly speak. And I didn't want her to. I didn't want her to say it, didn't want to hear it. I got up and crossed the room and shut my door in her face.

I knelt on my bed and looked out of the window and I saw the ambulance arrive. I don't think it was raining because I think I'd remember raindrops on the glass. I don't think it could have been sunny either because I don't think I had to shield my eyes. Maybe it was just a grey day. A nothing day. That would make sense. Although I want it to have been storming, with rain hammering, lightning splitting the sky, thunder shaking the house. But that wouldn't have been Dad. Dad was sunshine and music and laughter. But a hot day doesn't seem right either. Maybe one of those winter days that's so freezing you can see your own breath, but with bright sunshine making everything look new and exciting and possible. That's what kind of day it should have been. But I really don't think it was.

I hear a sound from inside – springs creaking and then Luke groaning. I hear the loo flush and water running in the bathroom, then water running in the kitchen and then he steps outside onto the balcony.

'Hey,' he says.

I look up at him. His hair is all mussed up and he still looks tired; his face is sort of unfocussed and his eyes are puffy.

'Hey. Did you sleep okay?'

He nods, scratching at the back of his neck. 'Not too bad. There was a spring in a delicate area at one point, but other than that . . . You?'

I nod. 'Yeah, I woke up suddenly, but apart from that it was fine.' And then I shake my head. 'Actually, no. I woke up and then I couldn't get back to sleep because I was thinking about what happened . . . with my dad.'

'I don't know what happened exactly,' Luke says. 'I mean, I don't know how . . . You don't have to tell me.'

'No, it's okay. He just died. In his sleep. He and Mum had gone out the night before for dinner with some friends and they came home and had a drink together – I was still awake when they came home, I heard them laughing. And I was thinking how lucky I was that they were so happy together, that they loved each other, that we were all happy as a family. And then when Mum woke up in the morning he was dead.'

My eyes fill with tears, as they always do when I say those three words.

'Did he have heart problems before?'

I shake my head. 'Never. It was just a massive heart attack. Nothing anyone could have done. He probably didn't even know.' My voice cracks. I hate thinking that he might have known, that he might have been scared. But the doctors kept telling us he wouldn't have known. I really hope that's true.

'I'm sorry,' Luke says. 'He was a lovely man.'

211

I smile even though I'm crying. 'He was. The loveliest. And he had all these plans. For himself. For all of us. I hate that he was so young and he's going to miss out on so much. I'm sorry,' I say, wiping my face with my fingers. 'Sometimes I can talk about him without crying and other times . . .'

'It's fine,' Luke says. 'You don't have to apologise.'

I take a breath. 'Do you know what I kept thinking about?'

Luke shakes his head, his eyes on mine.

'We used to watch *Grey's Anatomy* together. All of us. Dad loved it because he loved hospital dramas and he had a crush on Sandra Oh cos of that film, *Sideways*? And Mum always liked to talk about how ridiculous the medical details were. She'd sit there saying "That would never happen!" and we'd always say "It's not a documentary!"'

Luke smiles.

'And now he's never going to see it again. He's never going to know what happens to the characters. And I don't know either cos I can't stand to watch it without him. It seems so stupid thinking about a TV show when my dad's dead, but . . . I just know he'd be sad to be missing it.'

Luke nods. 'It was something you shared. It's okay to miss that.'

'Do you know what's even more ridiculous? I recorded the last season. I couldn't watch it, but I recorded it. In case he comes back.' I wipe my face again. 'I know he's not coming back. But I still can't believe it.'

Luke shifts in his seat so he's next to me and curls his arm around my shoulder. He strokes the back of my hand with his thumb.

'Do you want some tea? I'm going to make tea?'

'Tea would be good,' I say, sniffing.

While Luke's inside, I watch the early sun shimmering on the ocean in the distance and stretch my neck from side to side. When we left Rome and when we arrived here, I just wanted to get Leonie and go. But now I feel like I could stay. I don't know who I am without my dad. But I feel like it's time I started trying to work it out.

Luke comes back out with teas and sits down next to me. I relax against him, my forehead brushing his neck, and I just let myself breathe.

'Watching the sunrise?' he says.

I nod. 'Can't see it from here, but it's nice just watching the light changing. Mad to think it's setting now on the other side of the world.'

'I couldn't understand that when I was a kid,' Luke says. 'I thought it went and hid behind the horizon and then popped up again. I still kind of think that now.'

I smile at him and he leans forward and kisses me. He tastes like toothpaste. I want to climb into his lap, but there's plenty of time for that. Instead I press a few small kisses along his lips and sit back in my chair.

'I mean, I know the earth's revolving and the sun's not really moving . . .' he says as if he hadn't been interrupted. 'But I just don't buy it.'

'There's a lot of things like that,' I say. 'How planes stay in the air. They're metal. Metal's really heavy. It's impossible.'

'I still don't even get that the stars are still there in the day,' Luke says, shrugging.

'And we're all made of stardust,' I say. 'I just read about it in a magazine on the flight over. All the atoms in our bodies were once in stars.'

'I've read that too,' Luke says. 'It made my brain bleed.'

I nod. 'And it's in other people and things too. In everything. It's kind of incredible.'

'It really makes you think about how we're all part of something much bigger,' Luke says, before adding 'maaaan' in a hippy voice.

I smile at him and he smiles back at me, squinting a little against the watery sunlight.

And I know what I want to do with Dad's ashes.

23

It's busy at the harbour, so I don't expect to actually spot Leonie, but at the same time I have this image in my head of her standing still, everything and everyone bustling around her. In my overactive imagination she's brighter than everyone else and so I'll see her straight away. I don't, of course, but I do see someone who, for a second, I think is my dad. My stomach clenches and then I get that familiar feeling when I realise it can't be him, it can never be him again. But Leonie's here somewhere and I can't wait to see her.

I take out my phone and check it again.

'Nothing?' Luke says.

I shake my head. 'This feels like a film, don't you think? Like this is a trick?'

He laughs. 'I don't think it's a trick. She'll come and find us when she's ready.'

'I don't know what to do,' I say. 'I'm not good at waiting.'

I jump as my phone buzzes with a text. It's Leonie suggesting a pizza place for us to meet at.

'Public place so I won't make a scene,' I mutter, as I text

her back to say we're on our way. It's not far, just a bit further along the promenade, and it has huge windows looking out over the water.

I'm already looking for Leonie before we walk in and once we're inside, my stomach starts to flutter with nerves. What if she's not here? What if she's really not planning to come back with us to Rome?

She has to be here, she has to come. I can't go back to Rome without her.

'Milly?' I hear from behind me. I swing round and she's just coming through the doors. 'You got here first?' she says, her eyes wide, as she looks from me to Luke and back again. 'You must've been close.'

'I want to kill you!'

I grab her arms and pull her into a hug, feeling her press her face into my neck.

'I'm sorry,' she says.

'Are you okay?' I say, pushing her away again so I can look at her. It's only then that I see Gia standing outside, smoking and looking nervous.

Leonie looks fine. In fact, she looks great. She looks older than sixteen and much older than the picture I've had of her in my mind.

'I'm so sorry,' she says. 'I didn't want to worry you all.'

I shake my head. 'Seriously. Are you joking? What did you think would happen?'

She starts to speak, but we're interrupted by a waitress asking if we want a table. She shows us to a table at the front of the restaurant, in the corner, overlooking the beach.

'I hope you're paying,' I say to Leonie.

'I thought we could just get drinks,' she says. 'Maybe starters? Are you hungry?'

I shake my head. 'It's fine.'

She looks down at her hands on the table. 'I really am sorry.'

'Is Gia coming in?' I say, twisting in my seat to see if I can see her.

'No,' Leonie says. 'She's going back to work. She just wanted to make sure we met up, so she can tell her parents. I told them today and they were really upset.'

'About you and Gia?'

'No, they knew about that already. I told them how I left Rome. They were furious.'

'I don't blame them,' I say.

'Was Mum . . . Is Mum . . .' Leonie's eyes fill with tears.

'She's devastated, Leonie, what do you think?'

'I'm sorry. I just . . . I was already stressed about having to leave Gia, having to go home. And then when she was just so . . .' She shakes her head. 'I know I handled it really badly.'

'That's for shitting sure,' I say.

The waitress comes and we order some zucchini flowers and fried anchovies and artichokes and then Leonie says, 'Do you think Mum will forgive me?'

I kick her under the table. 'Of course she will, you stupid cow. Not sure about Elyse though.'

'Oh god,' Leonie says, looking out over the beach, her cheeks flushed and eyes still wet. 'Yeah, she's sent me a few menacing texts.'

'We were so worried,' I say, hooking my feet around her ankle. 'All of us.'

Leonie nods, looking back at me. 'I'm really sorry. Honestly. I don't know what I was thinking. It was like an out-of-body experience. And then once we got here . . . I felt I was in a dream. Like I could just sort of have this outside real life. Like here was separate and I didn't need to think about what was going on back in Rome.'

'I remember doing that when my dad left,' Luke says, fiddling with the napkin dispenser on the table. 'I would go somewhere – only, like, to the skate park or somewhere – and tell myself he was still at home, that he'd be there when I got back, and nothing had changed.'

'It's weird, right?' Leonie says, nodding, her eyes bright.

'I need to call Mum,' I say, unlocking my phone.

'Oh god,' Leonie says. 'I need to go to the loo. I'll be back in a minute.'

She jumps up, her chair scraping over the floor tiles, and dashes to the back of the restaurant. I actually start to get up to go after her, but realise I can't. I need to trust her. I tap on Mum's name on my phone and stare at the screen until I see her pick up.

'Is she really okay?' Mum says, once I've told her where we are.

'She's absolutely fine,' I tell her. 'She feels terrible though.'

'Does she . . . will she talk to me?' Mum asks and her voice sounds so small that my eyes fill.

'God, of course. She's just in the loo, hang on.' I suddenly have a vision of Leonie climbing out of the bathroom window and running away again and I shake my head to disperse it.

'Are you okay?' I ask Mum, as the waiter brings our food.

'Yeah. Alice is getting stressed about the wedding and I'm no help because all I can think about is. Leonie, but yeah. I'm fine.'

I see Leonie coming out of the bathroom. A waiter stops and says something to her, smiling wide, eyes twinkling, and she throws her head back and laughs before saying something back to him in, I think, Italian.

'Hang on, Mum,' I say, covering the phone.

'Were you just speaking Italian?' I ask Leonie as she gets closer.

Her cheeks go pink and she nods. 'Yeah. Gia's been teaching me.' She points at my phone. 'Is that Mum?'

I nod. 'Will you talk to her?'

She almost yanks the phone out of my hand. 'God. Of course!'

Leonie is crying and she's never been a quiet cryer, so I grab her elbow and steer her out of the restaurant. Once we're outside, I lead her over to the little wall that separates the promenade from the beach.

'I know,' Leonie says into the phone, her voice small and tight. 'Once we were out of Rome, I felt awful. Please don't –'

I turn back to the restaurant to give her some privacy, but see Luke coming outside and we both walk over to a stone bench just in front of the restaurant and sit down.

'Thank you,' I say, dropping my head down on his shoulder and looking over at my sister.

'What for?'

'Bringing me. Being here. Paying in there.'

'Didn't you pay?' he says. 'I thought you paid!'

I sit bolt upright and look at him, but he's already laughing.

'Dickhead,' I say, dropping my head back down again. 'Thank you.'

'No worries. I'm glad she's okay.'

I nod, my cheek sliding against the fabric of his T-shirt. It smells like fabric conditioner. Lemon. I turn my head a little and kiss the side of his neck, tasting salt and Luke Luke Luke.

Luke parks the car in the street behind San Georgio, turns off the engine and the three of us just sit there.

'I can't get out,' Leonie says, sighing. 'My legs are dead.'

'They are not,' I say.

'They are. Luke, can you pull up right in front of the restaurant and just push me out of the car?'

Luke laughs. 'Come on. You're fine.'

He opens his door and then turns to look at me. 'You're fine, right?'

I nod. But I feel nervous too. They're all waiting for us. It feels like a lot of pressure. And it feels like we've been away for a lot longer than two days. I get out of the car and walk around the back to open Leonie's door. I've only opened it a little when a guy on a moped buzzes past, swerving annoyingly close to the car, and I have to press up against it. The metal's hot, the sun glinting off the trim around the door and dazzling my eyes.

I duck down and look through the window at Leonie. She's looking back at me, her eyes wide and her face pale. I pull the door open.

'Come on,' I say. 'I'll hold your hand.'

'Promise?' she says, reaching out to me.

'Promise.' I grab both of her hands and half pull her out of the car.

'It feels like I've been away for ages,' she says, as we walk towards San Georgio, Luke behind us.

I nod. 'It really does.'

I look at the flower stall at the end of the square and beyond it to the hole-in-the-wall selling pizza bianca. Was it really only yesterday that I was eating pizza bianca with Luke at the services? I glance at him over my shoulder and feel him touch the small of my back with his fingers. It makes me shiver.

We're two shopfronts away from San Georgio when Leonie stops dead and turns to me.

'Thank you,' she says. 'For coming to get me. And for not yelling at me.'

'No problem,' I say. 'I think Elyse will do the yelling.'

She smiles. 'Yeah.' She looks at Luke. 'Thank you.'

'No problem,' Luke says, resting his hand gently on her shoulder.

'I can do this,' she says, taking a deep breath.

'You can do this,' Luke agrees.

'You really can,' I tell her.

And then we walk through the side door and into San Georgio.

24

Alice was right and everything is organised and calm on the morning of the wedding. The sun is shining, of course, and we all have breakfast together in the garden. Alice and Stefano can't stop smiling at each other and Stefano's *nonna*, Vera is literally hopping up and down with excitement.

After breakfast, we all go upstairs to get ready and we can hear guests arriving downstairs. Alice isn't having bridesmaids or anything so we're all just wearing our own clothes. Leonie's wearing a red sundress with ruffles from the top to the bottom. She puts her hair up and she looks so grown-up I can't quite believe it. When did it happen? I still picture her in her checked school summer dress. And next year she'll be the only one at home.

'Help me cover this,' she says to Elyse, pointing at another love bite on her neck.

'Bloody hell, Leonie,' Elyse says. 'Tell Gia to calm the fuck down.'

Leonie rolls her eyes. 'We had to have a proper goodbye. Are you going to help me or not?'

'Not,' Elyse says. 'Do it yourself.' She throws her enormous make-up bag onto Leonie's bed. Leonie sighs and unzips it, tipping almost everything out onto the cover.

'Jeezus!' Elyse says, tugging the bag back towards herself. 'A bit of respect, please.'

'Just do it for me,' Leonie says, blinking at Elyse. 'Please.'

'In a minute,' Elyse says. She's leaning over the console dressing table and doing her eyebrows in the mirror. She's wearing a mint-green lace dress that one of her friends from college made. It looks amazing on her. It's a bit twenties in style and she's fastened her long hair back.

I'm wearing a green and white fifties-style dress Elyse made for me. I hardly ever wear dresses at home and I'd looked and looked for one but couldn't find anything I liked at all. I really love this dress though. I feel like someone from an old film. And if I spin around, the skirt flares out.

'That looks so gorge on you,' Leonie says. 'How are you wearing your hair?'

'I was going to put it up,' I say and I hold it in a ponytail to show her.

She cocks her head on one side and squints at me. 'I think it looks better down with that dress, but it needs something. Ooh!'

She rummages in her bag and then clips my long fringe over to the side.

'I don't think so,' I say.

'Just look in the mirror. You look gorgeous.'

I stand next to Elyse and look in the mirror. I wouldn't say gorgeous, but the simple way my sister's clipped my hair has actually made all the difference. I worry that my forehead's too big when my fringe is off my face, but I don't think that now at all. And I think it actually makes my eyes look a bit bluer.

'I love it,' I tell Leonie. 'Thank you.'

She comes to stand next to me and we look at each other in the mirror.

'Look at us,' Leonie says, smiling.

Elyse puts down her eyebrow pencil and smiles at us in the mirror.

'I can't remember the last time we all got dressed up together,' I say.

The matching expression on my sisters' faces reminds me. It was Dad's funeral.

We meet Mum downstairs. She's wearing a long dark-pink skirt and a white shirt with her hair piled up on her head and she looks so beautiful. The restaurant looks incredible too. There are flowers on every surface and bowls of sugared almonds in little bags, along with tiny Iced Gem biscuits that Alice loves.

We all head outside and my mouth drops open when I see the garden. It's been transformed into a wedding grotto. We went to bed pretty late last night so either someone stayed up even later or got up much earlier because the trees are strung with multicoloured bunting and again there are flowers everywhere. Folding chairs entwined with flowers have been set out in rows facing the table under the weeping willow, where Stefano and Alice will sign the register. Even the table's been hand-chosen: it's white with bow legs and a multicoloured mosaic top.

'It's breathtaking, isn't it?' Mum says.

'So beautiful,' Elyse says and puts her hand up to her face.

'Are you crying?' Leonie says, laughing.

'Oh, shut up,' Elyse says.

We move to one side so we're not blocking the doorway, but carry on just staring at the garden.

'If you're crying now, I dread to think what you'll be like later,' I say.

'I've got tissues,' Mum says. 'I'm expecting a few tears. Alice has been crying already this morning.'

'Is she okay?' I ask.

'She's nervous,' Mum says. 'But she's happy too. She's been planning this for such a long time, I think it's all a bit overwhelming.'

Toby comes out with a platter of pastries and a pot of coffee and puts it on the big table by the wall. 'Help yourself,' he says, grabbing a pastry for himself.

'I thought you weren't working today?' I ask him.

He's wearing a black suit and white shirt with a napkin tucked down the front in case of spillages.

'That's me done. That was my last responsibility. Until, you know . . .' He gestures at the table. Toby is Stefano's best man.

'Is your mum okay?' Leonie asks.

Toby nods and then grins. 'She's stopped crying. Now she's holding ice to her eyes.'

I walk around the garden taking it all in. It looks like something from a dream. Or a film. I notice that the bunting actually has 'Stefano + Alice' printed on, along with the date. And the ice-cream colours of the bunting and the flowers match the mosaic on the top of the table (and, for that matter, Mum's skirt).

The next person through the door is Luke and my breath catches as soon as I see him. Like Toby, he's wearing a suit, but his is navy blue, and a white shirt that shows off his tan. He grins and heads straight over to me.

'You look beautiful,' he says, smiling.

'You too,' I say. 'Good, I mean. You look good.'

He grins. 'I was cool with "beautiful".' He reaches out and wraps his fingers around my wrist. I turn my hand so I'm holding his wrist too. I can feel his pulse under my fingers.

'So have you heard what Stefano and Alice want us to do?' Luke says, looking down at our hands.

'No. What?'

'They want us to walk down the aisle ahead of them. In pairs.'

I must look blank, because he adds, 'You know? Two by two.'

'Like the ark?' I say.

He laughs. 'Yeah, I guess. I think Alice is nervous about walking down the aisle with everyone looking at her or something.' He shakes his head. 'I don't really know. But there's me, Toby, Stefano's friends, Vincenzo and Marco, and your mum and the four of you. So . . .'

'And Alice told you to partner me?' I ask.

'No,' he says and smiles. 'I chose you.'

The sun is shining. Music is playing. My family all look beautiful – happy and confident. My Dad is conspicuous by his absence and I can't imagine how beyond hard this must be for Mum, watching her sister marrying the man she loves while the man my mum loves died in bed next to her.

226

But all I can think is 'I chose you.' Over and over. 'I chose you.' And it makes my insides do a happy little hop every single time, which is ridiculous since I know he's chosen lots of girls. And I'm here and he knows I like him and so it's the easiest thing in the world for him to choose me. But still I can't stop thinking about it.

The music for the ceremony starts and Luke arrives next to me. As Mum and Stefano's friend Vincenzo start walking, I feel like I can't quite catch my breath. I've never hyperventilated before – I've only ever seen it in films when they make people breathe into a paper bag – but I feel like I'm doing it now. Marco and Elyse start walking and I can hear myself panting like a dog. Toby and Leonie are behind us so we're next. And then Luke takes my hand.

We start walking and the 'I chose you' in my head has been replaced by a kind of whooshing sound. I'm breathing fine, so that's good, but I'm not thinking so well. And I can't stop smiling.

Luke and I are at the front now and we step to one side and sit down on the front row next to Mum and Vincenzo. Luke's still holding my hand, his thumb brushing over my knuckles, and he whispers 'Are you okay?' in my ear. I nod and smile at him. His eyes look almost gold in this light. I want to run my fingertips over his eyelashes.

Instead, I turn away and look down the aisle at Stefano and Alice. Stefano looks his usual gorgeous self in a black suit and a pink shirt, but Alice looks unbelievable. Her dress is full length and pure white. It's covered with lace and little jewels that glint in the sun. She's beaming. I don't think I've ever seen her look so happy, and Stefano can't stop looking at her. Once they reach the front the music stops and the ceremony starts.

After the ceremony is over, we all stand up and hug Stefano and Alice and, at some point, Luke lets go of my hand. Or I let go of his, I don't know.

We go inside for champagne and a few of Stefano's family make toasts while the staff move the folding chairs and bring more tables outside for the meal. I've finished my first glass and I'm wondering if I can get away with a second without getting drunk, sick, or falling asleep when Stefano comes in to announce that the garden is ready and the meal is served.

Our table has Alice and Stefano, Toby and Luke, Mum, Elyse, Leonie and me. Everyone takes their place, leaving me, Leonie and Luke. Leonie throws herself into the seat next to Elyse, and I sit next to Mum so that Luke is between me and Leonie. Once the waiters have been round and poured our drinks, Stefano stands up and raps his fork against the side of his glass. We all look up at him obediently.

'I'm not going to make a big speech,' he says, holding one hand up. 'No really. I want everyone to eat and drink and have fun. But I can't wait any longer to say how beautiful my wife looks . . .'

He has to stop talking while everyone cheers and claps and he beams down at Alice. Alice looks teary and her cheeks are bright pink.

'Yes,' Stefano says, when everyone's calmed down. 'My wife. I'm so proud to finally say that Alice is my wife. I love you, *tesoro mio.*'

Alice stands up and kisses him, her hand on his cheek. They both look so happy that I find myself welling up again. I glance over at Luke and he's looking at me. I give him a watery smile and he grins back.

'I know it's not customary for the bride to give a speech,' Alice says and everyone cheers. 'But I say what the hell, it's the twenty-first century and I would like to say a few things.'

Everyone cheers again, possibly even more than they did for Stefano, and Alice laughs.

'First, I want to thank my beautiful husband. I thank god . . . or the universe or whatever . . . every day that I met you. You're the love of my life and I know we're going to be just as happily married as we were unmarried.'

Stefano has sat back down and Alice leans over and kisses him again. The way he's looking at her makes my heart hurt.

'I've been very lucky in my life,' Alice says. 'I've got a lovely family . . . My wonderful little boy, Toby, who is growing up to be an amazing young man. And my beautiful sister, Carrie. Carrie's marriage to Dominic was . . .' She stops and shakes her head, closing her eyes, then says, 'I'm going to have to have a little drink if I'm going to be able to finish this.' She sips her Prosecco and I take the opportunity to drink some of mine too.

'Sorry,' Alice says, putting her glass down. 'Carrie's marriage to Dominic was my inspiration. They loved each other so much. They were best friends. They were incredible parents to my gorgeous nieces. It's really a tragedy that Dominic can't be here . . . although I can't imagine that he's not here, somewhere. So I wanted to make a toast to a few people.' She picks up her glass again and we all do the same. 'The family I feel blessed to have, and to Dominic.'

We all raise our glasses and say, 'To Dominic.'

I look at Mum and see that there are tears running down her face. Alice walks around the table and Mum turns around to hug her, before pulling back and saying, 'I don't want to get make-up on your dress!'

Alice laughs and I realise she's crying too. My throat is aching with the effort of not crying. I just don't want to cry now. It's all so beautiful and it's such a happy occasion. I don't want to miss Dad; I want to pretend that he's here, that's he's just gone inside for a drink or that he's over in the corner chatting to the band as they set up, asking them about their equipment and joking with them over their set list.

'Are you okay?' Luke asks me when the speeches are over.

I nod and then I feel his fingers on mine. I look down. I'm clinging to the edge of the table and I didn't even realise I was doing it. Luke gently prises my fingers away and slides his own fingers between them, squeezing my hand.

'Do you want to leave the other one?' he says and nods at my other hand, which is also holding on.

I reach out and pick up my glass. 'I'll just hold on to this,' I say, smiling.

He laughs. 'Not all night though. There's going to be dancing later, so you need to keep your wits about you. Toby's going to show us some moves.'

'Hey!' Toby says. 'I've got moves.'

'You have,' Luke says, nodding. 'But they're all tragic.'

'Oh, that's not true,' Alice says. 'Tobes used to know the dance routine to that Backstreet Boys song . . .'

'Thanks, Mum,' Toby says. 'That's really helpful.'

'Which Backstreet Boys song?' Luke asks, grinning.

'No. Thank you. This conversation is over,' Toby says. 'So . . . Mum, Stefano. Married, you say?'

Everyone laughs. Toby reminds me a bit of dad, the way he can always charm everyone. Probably why they got on so well.

I turn to Mum. 'Are you okay?'

She nods. Her eyes still look a bit wet, but her smile seems genuine. 'It was a beautiful speech,' she says. 'And everyone looks so happy and excited. I just wish he was here.'

After the incredible meal – five courses starting with antipasti and finishing with an ice-cream cake and limoncello shots – the band stops playing quiet background music and starts playing the stuff designed to get everyone up and dancing.

'What was that Backstreet Boys song?' Luke asks Alice, grinning. 'Maybe they know it.'

'Don't even think about it,' Toby says.

The band starts with 'Moondance' by Van Morrison – the band is Italian, but singing in English – and before they've even reached the first chorus, dozens of people are up and dancing as the staff hurries to clear the tables and move them to the edges of the garden.

The band have been on a break, but they start playing their second set and Leonie leans forward, looking past the others to me.

'What?' I say.

'I thought you might've changed your mind,' Leonie says.

'What about?' Elyse asks, looking from Leonie to me.

'Mum asked Milly to sing,' Leonie tells her.

I feel Luke's fingers on the back of my hand, sliding round to tangle with mine. I squeeze his hand without looking at him.

'You don't have to do it if you don't want to,' Elyse says.

'I know,' I tell her.

I look over at the band: five men, all dressed in black, arranged around one guy sitting down, playing the double bass. I think back to my band. The band I was in for two years before Dad died. I used to love being on stage with them, loved singing with them, loved the nerves before we played and how giddy we all were after. I miss it. But I don't think I can do it now.

'Why don't you go and talk to them?' Elyse says. 'See how you feel?'

I feel sick at the thought. Which almost certainly means I shouldn't do it. But if I do go to Liverpool, I'll have to sing in front of people all the time. Luke's other hand slides up my arm and I realise I'm squeezing his fingers.

'Sorry,' I say, glancing up at him.

'You don't want to do it,' he says.

I shake my head.

'So don't do it.'

I laugh. 'That simple?'

'Course,' he says.

The band start playing and it only takes me a few seconds to recognise 'Fly Me to the Moon'.

'Oh god,' I hear Elyse say.

'Fly Me to the Moon' was Dad's favourite song. He sang it on stage, he sang it at karaoke, he sang it around the house, he sang it at every family party ever.

I hear a sniff and look over to see that Leonie is crying, her face pressed against Elyse's neck.

'I remember your dad singing this,' Luke says. 'At Alice's barbecue.'

I shake my head. 'He didn't sing this that night. I would've remembered if it was this. He sang this all the time.'

'I was sure it was this,' Luke says.

Maybe it was. Maybe I blanked it out. Maybe Luke's remembering it wrong. I picture Dad standing in Alice's garden, laughing as he sang. Twirling a bit. Using whatever was to hand to pretend he had a microphone – barbecue tongs, a solar light he'd pulled out of the ground, his mobile.

I feel something building inside my stomach. It feels like nerves, but it also feels like excitement. I'm walking across the garden, my heels sinking into the grass, before I even have time to think about it.

The guy with the double bass – his name's Jaxon and I'm surprised to find he's American, not Italian – taps the microphone and says, 'We have a special treat tonight. Milly – Alice and Stefano's niece – is going to sing one of my favourite songs.'

A cheer goes up and I feel it inside my chest. I glance around a little and every face I see is smiling back at me. I tell myself that Dad is here with me.

The band starts to play the ridiculously familiar intro and I can feel Dad next to me. I feel it so strongly that I want to turn and smile at him, but I know that if I do look, he won't really be there. So I just start to sing instead.

The rest is a blur. It often happens when I'm singing; I just tune out of the world and into the music and let it carry me along. It's odd because I'm never this confident when I'm not singing and I hate having to do presentations at school, but when I'm singing it's like I just become part of the music and the other me – the me I am most of the time – steps to one side.

It's fine. Not amazing. My throat is tight and I forget some of the words and miss some of the notes, but it's fine. I focus on the fairy lights and the stars, the tiny birds darting overhead and the leaves on the trees.

My skin feels like it's vibrating. I feel alive. And that just seems so wrong to me. I'm alive and my dad's dead. And I wonder if this is why I've avoided singing. Not just because I knew how much it would make me miss him, but because I know that it makes me feel this way and I know it made Dad feel this way too and I don't want to feel like this when he can't.

My eyes skip past Leonie, Elyse, Toby and Luke to land on Mum, who is beaming at me, her hands clasped and pride written all over her face. I so desperately want to see my dad's face, but I picture him in my head instead. He would be proud. He was always proud. So many people have told me, but for the first time maybe ever, I can really feel it. And it feels like love.

25

As everyone gets up the following morning, we slowly gather in the garden. Someone has left pastries and coffee again, but it's not Stefano because he and Alice have yet to appear.

'Remember our first night here?' Mum says, her eyes closed, sun shining on her face.

Mum was already up when I came downstairs, Elyse and Leonie joining us not long after.

'It was a full moon and we made a wish?' Mum says, opening her eyes and shielding them from the sun.

I nod.

'What did you wish for?' Mum asks me.

'I wished for you to be happy again,' I say.

Elyse groans. 'I wished that Robbie was in love with me.'

'You knew he wasn't?' Mum asks her.

Elyse nods, smiling a little. 'I was pretty sure he wasn't, yeah. And if I couldn't just, you know, force him to be, I thought wishing might work.'

Mum gives Elyse a sad smile and drops an arm around her shoulder. 'I'm sorry.'

'It's okay,' Elyse says. 'I mean, it feels shitty right now, but why would I want to be with someone who doesn't want to be with me?'

'I wished I could tell you about Gia,' Leonie says, her voice small. 'About Gia and about wanting to study medicine and about wanting to have a year off in Italy first.' She laughs a little. 'All my secrets.'

'I'm so sorry,' Mum says again, reaching out and grasping Leonie's hands. 'And we can talk about all of that, okay? No more secrets.'

'No more secrets,' Leonie says, nodding.

'What did you wish for?' I ask Mum.

'Same as you really,' she says lightly.

'To be happy again?' I ask.

She shakes her head. 'Not quite. But to be happy that I'm still here. Even without him.'

'Fuck,' Elyse says.

Mum pushes at her, half laughing, but my throat is burning with tears and I'm scared that if I start to cry I'll end up sobbing.

'At work . . . I don't miss him,' Mum says, reaching out and taking my hand, keeping hold of Leonie's with her other hand. She takes a deep breath and Elyse leans against her shoulder. 'Because he was never there, I suppose. And because I'm so busy. And people know me for *me*. I can go hours and hours without thinking about him at all. At home it's . . . harder.'

Elyse nods. 'I think . . . I think it's sort of like what I wanted from Robbie. I wanted him to take me away from it.' She almost laughs, shaking her head. 'I mean, I know he couldn't, not really. I can't get away from it, I'll never be able to get away

236

from it. But when I was with him, I didn't think about it so much. And I almost felt like . . . if I could start my own life, my own adult life, my own home . . . it wouldn't hurt so much.'

'At L'Angelo,' I say, 'I couldn't think of a story about Dad that you didn't already know.'

'That's okay,' Mum says.

'No, I've got one now,' I tell her. 'We used to play "Name That Tune" in the car – he'd hum a bit of music and I had to guess it and then we'd swap. Did you all do that too?'

Leonie shakes her head. 'I never did that.'

'I think that was just you,' Elyse says.

I smile. 'Oh, and also once we went to Morrisons and bought a box of Magnums and we ate them all on the way home. Dad made me hide the box in next door's bin.'

Elyse laughs. 'Oh, we did that too. But with Tunnock's Teacakes.'

Leonie puts her hand up. 'Bag of Babybel.'

'Oh my god,' Mum says, laughing. 'He was terrible.'

'The worst,' I say, leaning my head against her shoulder.

'I'm sorry I didn't talk to you, any of you,' Mum says. 'I just didn't know how.'

I curl my fingers around hers and it feels so familiar but, at the same time, I can't remember the last time I did it. I can't remember the last time I held her hand.

'I felt at first like I needed to put on my own oxygen mask,' she continues. 'And then I'd be able to help you girls. But I just . . . I couldn't seem to get to a point where I felt like I was breathing on my own. And so I just left you all . . .'

'You didn't leave,' I say. Even though she hasn't been home much. We always knew she was coming back.

237

'I didn't leave physically, no. But I wasn't there for you. For any of you. And I regret it so much. I'm so, so sorry.'

All this time, I've felt like I had a rock inside me, like it was weighing me down and hollowing me out at the same time. And I finally feel like it's starting to crack and to crumble.

'That morning . . .' Mum starts and I flinch, jerking back in my chair. She reaches for my hand with her other hand, so she's holding one of mine with both of hers and she rubs my palm with her thumb. 'I'm sorry –'

'You don't have to –' I start, but she shakes her head, sadly.

'I do. I need to tell you how sorry I am. That I didn't help you. That I just left you to it. But I was . . . it was such a shock. I didn't know what to do. I didn't know where to start. I should have been stronger.'

I'm scared that if I try to speak I'll sob, so instead I shake my head. I manage to whisper, 'It's okay.'

'It's not,' Mum says. 'And I'm sorry.'

'I just miss him so much,' I say, tears rolling down my face.

'Me too,' Mum says, letting go of my hand and wiping my face. 'Me too, Milly.'

Leonie comes round from the other side of the table, and drapes herself over me and Mum, pressing her wet face into my neck. Elyse hugs Mum from the other side, grabbing a handful of my T-shirt.

'We've still got each other,' Mum says. 'We'll always have each other.'

Eventually, everyone joins us in the garden and there's an odd atmosphere – it's that in-between time when you know something is about to be over, but it's not over yet. So you can't quite let go, but you also can't hold on too tight.

Luke comes outside and sits on the chair next to me, running his knuckles down the back of my hand. I let go of the chair and tangle my fingers with his. If I'm going to hold on to something, I'd rather it was him.

'Can I call you when we get home?' he says, his mouth close to my ear.

'You'd better,' I say, turning to press a quick kiss to the corner of his lips.

'No PDAs, you two!' Leonie shouts from the other side of the garden, where she's talking to Alice and Stefano.

'That's a bit rich coming from the love-bite queen of Positano,' Elyse calls back.

'That's a love bite?' Mum says, scandalised. 'Oh, Leonie!'

I take my phone out and Luke puts his number in before ringing himself so he's got mine. When he hands me my phone back, I notice there's a WhatsApp notification from Jules. My chest feels tight – what if she doesn't want to be friends any more? What if I left it too long? What if she's pissed off at me? But her message says, 'I miss you too! So much. Are you at home?' I blink away tears as I tell her that I'm in Rome and I add again that I'm sorry. I can see straight away that she's replying and I hold my breath until her message appears: 'Don't worry. I understand. Love you. Come for Friday tea as soon as you're home. We all miss you so much.'

I put my phone back in my pocket and run my fingers around the edge of the pot containing Dad's ashes.

'You okay?' Luke says.

I nod. 'I just . . . I want to do a thing and it's a bit weird and I don't know how to ask.'

Luke waggles his eyebrows at me. 'Is it the hard hat thing, because I –'

'Oh my god! No!' I take the pot out of my pocket and hold it up.

'Is that Dad?' Elyse says, coming to sit down on the other side of me.

I nod. 'I want to sprinkle him here.'

Leonie crosses the garden too, sitting down on Elyse's other side. 'I poured mine into the ocean in Positano.'

I lean forward to look at her. 'Did you?'

She nods. 'I felt like it was time. It was beautiful.'

I close my eyes and listen to the leaves whispering above me. Luke squeezes my hand.

'I'm keeping mine,' Elyse says. 'For luck.'

I laugh. 'Is it windy enough, do you think? I don't want any, you know, blowback.'

Elyse licks her index finger and holds it up to the air. 'I think as long as you get the direction right.'

'Right,' I say.

'And maybe stand somewhere high,' Leonie adds.

'Okay.'

Luke drags one of the patio tables over into the garden and I step on a chair and then up onto the table. I look down at the faces of my family, all looking back up at me. I don't have anything to hold on to, but Luke's hand is wrapped around one of my ankles. I unscrew the top of the pot and put the lid in my pocket, then I hold the pot up over my head. For a few seconds nothing happens, but then the wind catches and the ashes start to swirl up into the air. They looked grey in the pot, but they're silver in the early morning sunlight.

I close my eyes and tip my face up to the sun.

Acknowledgements

I am so lucky to be able to do this for a job and I'm even luckier to be able to do it with so many fabulous and funny women. Thank you as always to my amazing agent, Hannah Sheppard; my wonderful editor Georgia Murray; and fabulous copy editor, Jenny Jacoby. Thanks and love to Rachel Lawston for the most glorious cover; Ilaria Tarasconi for double-checking my Italian; and everyone else at Hot Key.

All the love as always to the Sisterhood, Manatees, and Wordcount Warriors, with an extra bit for Keren David, Sophia Bennett and Susie Day for reading early drafts of this book and not telling me to chuck it out. (Although Keren did tell me to get rid of all the toast.)

Grazie mille to Luisa Plaja for Italian advice and feedback. Any mistakes are obviously mine.

An Aperol Spritz for Stella for leaping at the chance to show me Rome (even with a knackered back) and to Craig for finding (and paying for!) the perfect hotel. Where are we going next?

Hugs and a bit of inappropriate touching for my group chat faves, Alicia, Georgie, Jenni, Kevin and Lindsay.

Anything and everything else is for David, Harry and Joe. I couldn't do any of this without you.

Keris Stainton

Keris Stainton was born in Winnipeg, Manitoba, which, by all accounts, is very cold. And also hot. But when she was four months old, her parents moved back to the UK, and now she lives in Lancashire with a fellow northerner, their two ridiculously gorgeous sons and a pug. Okay, they haven't got a pug, but Keris hopes if she writes it here it will come true. If you write it, pugs will come.

Keris has been writing stories for as long as she can remember, but she didn't write a novel until 2004 when she took part in National Novel Writing Month. She hasn't quite finished that one yet, but she has finished a few others, including *Counting Stars*, *Jessie Hearts NYC*, *Della Says: OMG!*, and *Emma Hearts LA*. Find out more about Keris at www.keris-stainton.com or follow her on Twitter: @Keris

HOT
KEY
BOOKS

Thank you for choosing a Hot Key book.

If you want to know more about our authors
and what we publish, you can find us online.

You can start at our website

www.hotkeybooks.com

And you can also find us on:

We hope to see you soon!

Want to read
NEW BOOKS
before anyone else?

Like getting
FREE BOOKS?

Enjoy sharing your
OPINIONS?

Discover

READERS FIRST

Read. Love. Share.

Get your first free book just by signing up at
readersfirst.co.uk